FIRESTORM!

Also by Joan Hiatt Harlow

Secret of the Night Ponies

Blown Away!

Midnight Rider

Thunder from the Sea

Shadows on the Sea

Joshua's Song

Star in the Storm

FIRESTORM!

JOAN HIATT HARLOW

Margaret K. McElderry Books
NEW YORK   LONDON   TORONTO   SYDNEY   NEW DELHI

MARGARET K. MCELDERRY BOOKS

An imprint of Simon & Schuster Children's Publishing Division

1230 Avenue of the Americas, New York, New York 10020

MARGARET K. MCELDERRY BOOKS is a trademark of Simon & Schuster, Inc.

For information about special discounts for bulk purchases, please contact Simon & Schuster Special Sales at 1-866-506-1949 or business@simonandschuster.com.

The Simon & Schuster Speakers Bureau can bring authors to your live event. For more information or to book an event, contact the Simon & Schuster Speakers Bureau at 1-866-248-3049 or visit our website at www.simonspeakers.com.

Also available in a Margaret K. McElderry Books hardcover edition

Book design by Mike Rosamilia

The text for this book is set in Adobe Garamond Pro.

Manufactured in the United States of America

0811 OFF

First Margaret K. McElderry Books paperback edition September 2011

2 4 6 8 10 9 7 5 3 1

The Library of Congress has cataloged the hardcover edition as follows:

Harlow, Joan Hiatt.

Firestorm! / Joan Hiatt Harlow. — 1st ed.

p. cm.

Summary: A twelve-year-old street urchin and the son of Chicago's most important jeweler strike up an unlikely friendship in the days before the Great Chicago Fire of 1871, and both are nearly trapped when the city goes up in flames.

ISBN 978-1-4169-8485-6 (hc)

ISBN 978-1-4424-0979-8 (eBook)

[1. Social classes—Fiction. 2. Pickpockets—Fiction. 3. Poverty—Fiction. 4. Family life—Illinois—Chicago—Fiction. 5. Great Fire, Chicago, Ill., 1871—Fiction. 6. Fires—Illinois—Chicago—Fiction. 7. Chicago (Ill.)—History—To 1875—Fiction.] I. Title.

PZ7.H22666Fi 2010

[Fic]—dc22

2010012073

ISBN 978-1-4169-8486-3 (pbk)

This one's for

Sam,

one-year-old

Samuel Richard Balas

ACKNOWLEDGMENTS

THANK YOU to . . .

. . . Sarasota County Florida Public Libraries. What would I do without you and the great books you have available for history buffs like me?

. . . Chicago Historical Society, for your comprehensive archives and website.

. . . Myakka River Animal Clinic. Thanks to Dr. Dawn and her staff for information on goats and for letting me bond with Zeus, Bianca, Hansel, and Gretel. I ♥ goats! And many more thanks for the kind and loving care you show all animals—including my cats, Bubba and Amber.

. . . my writing group in Sarasota, Georgia, and New

Jersey—June, Gail, Betty, Elizabeth, and Carol—dear friends who have encouraged me on over the years and over the miles.

. . . my huge extended family—whether related to me or not! Thank you for your encouragement, understanding, and enthusiasm.

. . . my talented, gracious, and patient editors, Alexandra Cooper and Emily Fabre.

. . . my loyal fans who have been waiting for this story. Here you go!

CONTENTS

CHAPTER ONE

- Poppy -

Poppy sat up on her bare mattress and coughed. The stone walls and dirt floor of the room were closing in on her and she couldn't stop gasping for breath.

"Shut up!" Ma Brennan yelled from her bed across the room. "You're keepin' me and my girls awake."

"I . . . can't . . . help . . . it." Poppy's mouth was dry and her throat sore. It was hard to speak, and each word was interrupted by spasms of coughs.

Ma got out of bed and stomped toward Poppy. "I said *shut up!*" She grabbed Poppy by the shoulder with one hand and slapped her hard on the back with the other. "Not another sound out of you," Ma warned in the threatening whisper that Poppy had learned to fear.

Ma clomped back to her bed. Poppy's eyes watered as she buried her face into her unwashed pillow, trying to smother another fit of coughing.

Other sounds that echoed throughout the passage-ways of the old foundations didn't seem to bother Ma—the noise of men's rough laughter and cheers, a woman singing a rowdy song from the nightclub above them, snarling dogs fighting in the pits. Everything reverber-ated through the maze of hallways.

"You should be thankful to live here at the Willow," Ma often said to the girls.

The full name, "Under the Willow," sounded nice. A huge old willow tree spread its branches from the wet, muddy land near the Chicago River. The ground in Chicago was always damp, so the city officials had decided to raise the level of the streets. Old buildings and foundations, which couldn't be lifted, were empty. It wasn't long before a man named Roger Plant and his wife claimed owner-ship of the deserted foundations along Wells Street and rented out the vacant cellar rooms to all sorts of criminals and tramps. It was Plant who named one place Under the Willow and called it a "resort." He loved the old willow tree and watered it each day with a bottle of beer.

Ma Brennan had rented a room in the foundation and opened her school for girls, which right then consisted of Poppy and Ma's own daughters, Sheila and Noreen. What they learned at Ma's school was how to find a good "mark"—someone who was busy and unwary. Then Poppy or one of the other girls would slip close and pick his pocket, bringing the loot back to Ma.

Why is she so mean to me? Poppy asked herself. *I'm better at stealin' than her own kids. I can pick a pocket so smooth . . . and didn't I just bring her a leather full of dough yesterday?*

Poppy had hoped for a coin—a nickel, maybe—that she could have spent in a real store. But Ma had just popped the money into her own pocket and given her a nod. *Huh!* If it had been Sheila or Noreen bringing home a wad that big, she'd have treated them to ice cream.

Poppy rolled over and took the pillow off her face. She'd stopped coughing but couldn't get back to sleep. She heard a woman's scream from one of the chambers, then laughter. *Will I have to live here all the rest of my life?* Poppy wondered.

Ma always said Poppy should be grateful to have a bed and room here at Under the Willow. After all, her own mother didn't want her. She'd just dropped Poppy off in the alley when she was about four years old, and Poppy never saw her again. That was eight years ago, and that's when Ma took her in and gave her a place to live and taught her how to steal. Since then, other girls had come and gone, but Poppy still stayed on with Ma and her daughters.

Poppy was twelve now and good at what she did. She and the sisters were the ones who demonstrated to other "students" how to steal without getting caught. But after the others learned their craft, they went out on their own. So it was just Poppy, Sheila, and Noreen right now who made money for Ma. But Ma took everything.

Why should Ma get all the money, when I'm doin' the hard work? Well, not anymore! she decided. *I'll save some money from my marks and hide it somewhere. Then I'll get away from Ma Brennan. I'll live in a fine house in a nice neighborhood— and maybe even have a real family . . .*

A real family? Who'd want a guttersnipe like Poppy? Still, even living in a boat out on the lake with fresh clean air and lots of fish to eat would be better than this place. Maybe someday she'd sneak on board that steamer——the

Highland—and she'd end up somewhere far, far away from this smelly city with its stockyards.

She shuddered, remembering that visit to the stockyards when she'd been about five. That awful day Ma had taken her there to stand with the blood up to her ankles, making her watch the squealing hogs hanging on hooks—and then listening to the awful silence after the hogs were killed.

"This is what happens to bad girls," Ma had said. "Those who don't obey their mothers."

If Ma knew Poppy was planning to run away, Ma would whip her—or even something worse. Poppy cringed, recalling the hogs in the stockyard.

She'd need to be really careful and keep small amounts of money from her marks. Where would she hide her secret money? Maybe in a hollow tree, or in the ground. Maybe . . . Poppy was getting sleepy. Her eyes closed, and slowly she fell asleep holding her pillow to her face again.

It seemed as if she'd been asleep only a few moments when Poppy felt Noreen Brennan batting at her head. "Get up! It's Saturday, so we got to get out on the street early." Noreen was the same age as Poppy but looked a lot older. Poppy was small and looked younger than she really was. People seemed to like Poppy, and sometimes they'd give her a penny or a nickel just because she looked cute.

"I'm comin'." Half-asleep, Poppy placed her bare feet on the cold dirt floor. She knew if she lingered in bed, Ma would whop her.

"Somethin' smells good," Noreen's sister, Sheila, said with a loud sniff. "Ma's cookin' sausage." Sheila was fourteen, and Ma had put her in charge of the other two girls.

Poppy shivered as she washed her face in a pan of icy water. She pulled a dingy blouse over her head, then stepped into a skirt and tugged it up over her long drawers. After brushing her brown hair with the family brush, she ran with the other girls to the basement kitchen that several boarders shared. Only a few other people were in the room—most of them men who looked grimy and were probably heading out to rob someone. The whole complex of foundation rooms at Under the Willow was filled with thieves, gamblers, and drifters.

"About time," Ma yelled as the girls found a place at a table. She tossed a few slices of sausage along with a piece of bread onto tin plates and then slapped the dishes down in front of them.

"I'm expectin' a big bag o' sugar today, girls," Ma said. "Sugar" in Ma's language meant stolen money. "So the three of ya make up your mind who'll be the hook and who'll be the stalls, just like I taught ya. And choose nice, with no arguin' between ya."

Usually the three girls worked together picking pockets. Saturdays were good to find marks, since stores, banks, and the farmers' market were usually crowded on Saturday mornings.

The best place to find a prospect was near a bank, where a man or woman would have just cashed a weekly paycheck. Then Sheila, Noreen, and Poppy would begin the trick Ma had taught them: one or two would stall the victim by diverting his or her attention, while the hook picked the mark's pocket.

"I choose bein' the hook today," Poppy said before anyone else could speak. She wanted to start her plan to save money right away. By being the hook, she might be able to slip some of the money into her stocking or shoe before they gave it all to Ma.

"Well, I hope you can run faster than you did yesterday," Noreen said. "You almost got caught."

"I can run faster than you," Poppy snapped. "Besides,

I *never* get a chance to be the hook. I'm always skippin' rope or cryin' or somethin' to draw attention to *me*."

"That's 'cause you're littler than Noreen," Sheila argued. "Everyone thinks Poppy's so *cute*, with her *big brown eyes* and *long curls*." Her voice rang with sarcasm.

"Stop the arguin' and be *nice*, like I said before," Ma yelled, "or I'll do the choosin'."

"Yeah, shut up," one of the other boarders grunted. "I got a headache listenin' to ya."

"All right," Sheila whispered. "Since Poppy chose bein' the hook first, then Noreen and I will be the stalls."

"And I'll be the skipper this time," Noreen agreed, rolling her eyes. "O' course, I'm not half as *cute* as *Poppy*."

Ma pointed to the door. "Off you go and bring me a surprise like good girls."

The wooden sidewalks were crowded with pedestrians carrying bags of vegetables from the farmers' market. The harvest was bleak this year because of the drought. Fields of tomatoes and corn wilted in the sandy dust. Crops were small and wasted. Still, it was time to prepare for winter, so the market was bursting with activity.

Other people busied themselves with weekend errands to banks and shops along the way.

Sheila walked innocently along the road through the stalls where the farmers had set up their produce. She moved to the stores and banks that lined the sidewalks, searching for the right mark.

Noreen skipped rope back and forth on the walkway and dirt road, stopping and starting, bumping into folks occasionally. Some people looked at her icily.

Then Sheila signaled to Poppy with a quick flash of her thumb. A well-dressed woman had just left the General Bank. Sheila began following the lady, a little ways behind, until the other girls caught up.

Noreen, who was on the street skipping rope, hopped up onto the walkway, still skipping. She made her way ahead of the stylish lady. Sheila tapped her own left hip, which told Poppy that the money was in the woman's left pocket. Then Sheila casually sauntered inconspicuously nearer and nearer to the woman.

Poppy took a deep breath and headed closer.

In a flash Sheila pushed by the woman just as Noreen skipped into both of them.

The lady stumbled and Sheila held her by her right

arm. "Sorry, ma'am," she said. "That girl skippin' rope got right in my way!"

Noreen, still keeping the woman's attention away from Poppy, stuck out her tongue, then skipped off in another direction.

During this scuffle, without being observed, Poppy slipped two fingers into the woman's pocket and deftly pulled out a small package. Then, as swift and silent as a shadow, she tucked it under her blouse. Casually but quickly, she made her way down the sidewalk, hoping no one had seen her.

"You little urchin!" the woman called out after Noreen, unaware that she had just been robbed.

Poppy continued down the sidewalk through the crowd. She was already a good distance away from the skirmish. Crowds brushed one another, their shoes click-clacking on the timber sidewalk, oblivious to the robbery that had just taken place.

Has the woman realized her money is gone yet? Poppy wondered. Curiosity got the best of her. She peeked over her shoulder. Farther up the sidewalk, the lady she had frisked started screaming. "I've been robbed!" her voice carried throughout the crowd. People gathered around her as she pointed in Sheila's direction. Noreen had disappeared.

Then the lady looked straight at Poppy. Would she recognize her as the pickpocket?

Poppy, still looking over her shoulder, began to run when *SLAM!* She crashed into a boy who was sweeping the sidewalk outside a watch and jewelry store.

"Look what you did," he yelled, giving her a shove. "You knocked over my dustpan, and now everything is dirty again!"

"Sorry," she snapped. She slipped into the entryway between the two show windows of the shop, to conceal herself from the angry crowd up the street.

"What do you want here?" the boy growled. "This is an expensive jewelry store, and it's no place for the likes of you."

"Is that how you treat your customers?" Poppy drew herself up importantly. "I'm looking for a gift for . . . my mother."

CHAPTER TWO

- Justin -

Justin waved to his mother, who stood in the kitchen door of their big white colonial house. He paused for a moment and looked with satisfaction at the little goat shed he had built. He had just painted it red with a neat white trim around the door and window. The white picket fence and gate that surrounded the enclosure looked pretty on the lawn at the side of the house. And tomorrow he'd bring home the kid that Grandpa had promised him.

He ran down the long driveway that led to the street. Across the road a field of dry grass looked golden as it rippled in the morning breeze. He paused to catch his breath, then turned toward the two-mile walk to downtown State Street, where his father's jewelry store was located.

Father said if I helped at the shop and showed I was dependable, we'd pick up my goat tomorrow. And today of all days I had to go and get up late. Justin hurried along.

It was hot and dry, and Justin could taste the dirt that was stirred up as he ran toward town. When he approached the stable where their horse, Ginger, was boarded, he paused to catch his breath again. Should he take the horse? No, in the time it would take to get her ready, he could make it to the shop.

It was Saturday morning and the city of Chicago was just waking up. Horses pulling carts of vegetables from the prairie farms crowded the dirt streets to the farmers' market, stirring up dust clouds along the way. There had been no rain for months, it seemed, and dust was everywhere.

Justin never wanted anything as much as he wanted that cute little kid. Why, he'd been at the farm when she was born, and every time he went to his grandfather's, that baby goat followed him all over the place, bleating softly, her little tail wagging like the second hand on a watch.

Ticktock. That's what I'll name her.

He reached the family's jewelry store just as the clocks inside began to chime nine o'clock. The big broom, dustpan, and trash barrel were already outside the door, and Justin knew what his father wanted him to do without asking. He set to work first by brushing away dust from the wooden sign on the front of their store, just as his father came out. The winds had blown so much dirt from the dry earthen road that the painted gold words, BUTTERWORTH'S JEWELS AND TIMEPIECES, could hardly be seen.

Justin's father pointed to a cluster of dirt that had gathered under the roof of the entrance. "Don't forget to sweep near the door, son. The wind has piled the dirt up like drifting snow." Father locked the door. "In case anyone comes, I'll be back by the time you finish—about fifteen minutes." He walked up the street toward his favorite café, where he met Mr. Palmer every morning for coffee.

Justin moved into the entry and began to sweep when *SMASH!* A girl racing down the wooden sidewalk suddenly turned into the entrance and collided with Justin. "Look what you did," he complained, giving her a shove.

"You knocked over my dustpan, and now everything is dirty again!"

"Sorry." She glanced at the display of jewelry in the window. Justin looked at her tattered skirt and grimy blouse and knew she couldn't possibly shop at such an expensive store. He told her so.

"Is that how you treat your customers?" The girl stood haughtily. "I'm looking for a gift for . . . my mother."

Indeed! This girl was definitely not a customer! "We don't have anything you can afford," Justin said, picking up his dustpan.

"How do you know that?" The ragamuffin had her hands on her hips and her head cocked defiantly. "How do you know how much money I have?" She turned away to leave, but after peering down the street again, she moved back into the shelter of the entry. "How much is that necklace?" she asked, pointing to a pink cameo on a gold chain on display in the store window.

"Too much." Justin tried to sweep around her feet. "Move away."

"I asked you, how much?"

Justin sighed, looked closely at the small tag attached

to the necklace. "The price tag says one hundred and fifty dollars."

"It ain't that pretty," she snapped.

"The cameo is hand carved."

"It ain't got jewels on it. You ain't got jewels in this whole window," she scoffed, gesturing at the showcase. "This is just gold and silver. I don't believe there's a jewel in the store."

"Don't be stupid. We don't put jewels out here. We keep our jewels in the safe in the back room."

"So this is your family's store?"

"Yes. My name's Justin Butterworth—like on the sign."

The girl's brown eyes grew large. "So, you're tellin' me there's real sparkly kind of jewels in there? I ain't never seen a real honest-to-goodness ruby . . . or diamond. Where'd you get them?"

"From around the world—emeralds from Colombia, diamonds from Africa . . ."

"How come we don't have jewels here in Chicago?"

"'Cause precious stones don't grow here."

"What do you mean 'grow'? Stones don't grow. I'm not stupid, Justin."

"They do so grow. They grow in the ground."

"Well, who plants them in the first place?"

"Nobody plants them! They just grow on their own. It takes millions of years." He thought of his geode collection. "I have rocks with gems growing out of them, right in the back room here."

"Show me."

"Well, I don't have the key or I'd prove it."

"I guess your father doesn't trust you very much, if he won't even let you have a key." She went to the sidewalk and looked up the street again. Then she returned to Justin. "So does your pa pay you for sweepin'?"

"That's none of your business."

The girl ignored him. "I'll bet you're only about . . . twelve."

"I'm thirteen. Who are you, anyway?"

"Poppy," she answered. "I'm twelve."

"Poppy . . . what? Don't you have a last name?"

"No. I never knew my folks. Just call me Poppy. That's what everyone else calls me."

Justin stopped sweeping. "Well, if you haven't got folks, why are you lookin' for a gift for *your mother*?"

Poppy sniffed and stuck up her nose. "I live with

my . . . aunt. She's like a mother. But I don't need anyone to take care of me." She looked at Justin more closely. "It looks like you have to work, however—even though your father owns the store and all."

"Father promised me that if I helped him on a regular basis and showed I'm dependable, I'd be able to have a pet." *Why am I even talking to this guttersnipe, anyway?* He started sweeping again, blowing the dust up in angry swirls.

"What kind of pet?"

"A goat," Justin answered without stopping.

Poppy threw back her head and burst out laughing. "You want a *goat*?"

"Yes. A goat! Why not?" he snapped. "Is that so strange?"

"I'd rather have a kitten than a goat for a pet. Where would you get it?"

Justin sighed. *Is there any way to get rid of this girl?* "My grandpa's goat had two kids. One is sold, and Grandpa told me I could have the other one." He gestured to the street. "Isn't your mother . . . *aunt* looking for you?"

Poppy ignored Justin's question. "Goats don't make good pets." She clamped her fingers on her nose. "And goats stink."

"My grandpa's goats do *not* stink!" Justin threw down the broom. "That's 'cause they're taken care of, and washed and brushed and fed and . . . loved. And from the looks of you, no one loves you very much, or you'd be washed and brushed and fed and . . ."

"Loved." She turned away and looked up at the roof, her head cocked in a sassy sort of way.

Maybe she'll leave now, Justin hoped. *Father would be upset if he knew this little tramp has been hanging around our store.* Justin began scooping up dirt with the dustpan and throwing it into the trash bin.

"How can you love a goat?" Poppy asked, still looking away.

"It's easy. She runs to me when I go visit, and her tail wags like the second hand on a pocket watch. In fact, I'm going to name her Ticktock." When Poppy snickered and rolled her eyes, Justin added angrily, "I'll prove it to you if you come back on Monday. We're getting Ticktock on Sunday and I'll be here on Monday afternoon after school. I'll bring her with me. You can see for yourself what a great pet she is."

Poppy stood still, staring at him. She didn't speak for a long moment. Then she said, "Well, if you bring your goat on Monday, I'll come to see her."

"All right," Justin answered.

"You can show me those jewels, too—the ones that grow in the ground. If you can get a key, that is." Poppy looked cautiously up and down the street, then walked off onto the crowded sidewalk.

She'll never show up on Monday, Justin thought. *She was hanging around here only 'cause she's scared of someone. That's why she kept looking up the street.* Still, he wanted to prove that he had a goat and that his father trusted him with a key. Then he'd show her his geode collection and prove to her that jewels really did grow in rocks.

Justin finished cleaning the entry and the sidewalk just as his father came into sight.

Whew! Poppy left in the nick of time! he thought.

CHAPTER THREE

- *Poppy's Secret* -

Poppy started down the sidewalk, still wary of anyone who might have seen her steal the lady's money. But the clamor had subsided, so it seemed safe now to head home. She reached under her blouse to feel the packet she had stolen. The woman must have just cashed a check in the bank, for Poppy could tell it was all crisp new bills—the kind the government had printed during the war. Ma would be happy with her take that day. *But what about me?* Poppy wondered. She had risked getting arrested and put in jail for stealing. She had every right to take her share of what she had stolen, hadn't she?

Yes, she'd carry out her plan to save some of the sugar for herself—for when she'd run away and start her own life without Ma and the girls telling her what to do. But first she had to find a spot to hide the money—someplace near the Willow, but out of the way enough where no one else could find it.

As she turned down a side road to Clark Street, she heard the clang of loud bells. Two horses pulling a fire engine came racing up the road. The sound of steam and the clopping of horses' hooves resounded loudly on the dry, hard street. The engine turned onto the next street and sped beyond the run-down buildings. Poppy could see a spiral of smoke swirl its way up into the clouds.

Another fire! *Seems like there's at least one fire every day. If we don't get rain soon, the whole town may burn up,* Poppy thought.

After she passed a line of deserted, dilapidated houses, she approached an empty lot not too far from the Willow. A building had been moved away to comply with the town's demand to raise the level of the city streets. The rock foundation was crumbling and the land was filled now with dry weeds, grass, and dandelions. A few small trees reached up to the sky with leafless limbs. Fall had come early this year because of the drought.

Maybe there'd be a place in there to hide my loot. Poppy crossed the street and looked around to see if anyone was watching her. The large lot was filled with old newspapers, bottles, and other junk that was partly covered with dead leaves. She shuffled through the debris and closer to the stone foundation.

I've got to find a space where I can keep what's mine, where no one would suspect there's anything there.

Poppy glanced over her shoulder again, to make sure no one was around, and then bent down to the stone wall that had once been the foundation for the building. The cement that had previously held the rocks together had crumbled away and the stones all looked alike—except for one gray rock that sparkled with pieces of shiny stuff.

Poppy wiggled it, and almost immediately the stone fell out and into her hands. Poppy suddenly recalled what Justin had told her—that jewels grew in rocks. She examined the bits of tiny sparkles on this stone. Were they diamonds? If they were, they were very small. And Justin said diamonds didn't grow in Chicago.

She reached into the opening up to her elbow, and she could feel another stone at the end of the cavity. Good! Even if someone removed the rock, the money would be way back in the hole. This was the perfect spot for her getaway stash!

Poppy kicked around at the junk beneath her feet and came across an empty can that was fairly clean inside. Then she removed from under her blouse the bank envelope she had stolen. Twenty-five dollars in five-, two-, and one-dollar bills were folded neatly inside. *Ma won't notice if I take five dollars. She'll still have twenty, and that's more than the other girls bring in with just one boodle.*

Poppy folded two two-dollar bills and one one-dollar bill and put them into the can. Then, glancing around once more, she slipped the can into the hole and replaced the rock.

After putting the rest of the money under her blouse again, she ran back across the street—and stopped.

Noreen was waiting for her. "What were you doing over there?" she asked suspiciously.

"Er . . . nothing. I thought I saw a stray cat. So I went over to see it."

Noreen didn't speak for a long minute. Then she shrugged her shoulders. "You and your cats," she said. "Ma would never let you keep a cat . . . or a kitten. So just forget it."

"It's all I want . . . a little kitten."

"Where we live is no place for a little kitten. Someone would probably kill it if they saw it at the Willow."

"Someday I'll have a kitten," Poppy said. "Even if I have to move away."

"Come on, let's go home." Noreen started up the road.

Poppy walked fast to keep up with her, wondering if Noreen really hadn't seen her put the money into the secret hiding place.

When they arrived at the Willow, the resort was filling up with boisterous men and women, beginning another evening of drinking and carousing. How Poppy hated going down the dark stairway that led to the cellar foundation where she lived! Even when the sun shone brightly outside, she had to enter this darkness every night as she returned to Ma Brennan's place.

Sheila and Ma were already there, and before Poppy could enter the room, Ma grabbed her by the arm and pulled her inside. "Where have you been? Where's the money?"

"Right here," Poppy replied angrily, reaching under her shirt. "Give me a minute, will ya?"

Ma gave a quick, sharp slap across Poppy's face. "How many times have I told you not to back talk?"

Poppy didn't answer, but her hand shook as she handed the money to Ma. If Ma knew she had taken some of it, what would she do to Poppy? She'd give her more than a slap in the face. That was certain.

Poppy stood with her head down as she waited for Ma to count the bills.

"Good! This is what I need to feed the three of you!" Ma spoke with the pained voice she used each time she took money from the girls. "It won't pay for *my* meals, but I'm not thinkin' of myself, as usual. I'll get by." Poppy looked away. Twenty dollars was enough to buy food for the family for a month. Poppy knew it was a trick of Ma's to make her look as if she were giving up so much for her girls.

"Oh, Mama, you mustn't sacrifice for us," Sheila whimpered. "You need to eat and stay well."

"We'll *all* get by," Noreen agreed, and went to her mother's arms. "Poppy is lucky to be part of our family . . . even though she isn't really one of us." She gave Poppy a long look, and Poppy wondered again if she had seen her putting the money away.

Ma interrupted Poppy's thoughts. "Hush, Noreen!" said Ma. "Poppy's like a sister to you. Besides, look what she brought us today. There's twenty dollars in here!"

Ma counted the money again, then patted Poppy's arm. "Sorry I had to slap ya, Poppy. But your ma has got to discipline ya once in a while—to teach you respect."

Poppy nodded, but inside, her desire to get away was stronger than ever. Still, how would a measly five dollars now and then make it possible to run away?

Suddenly she remembered that boy, Justin, the one whose father owned the jewelry store on State Street— the one who'd promised to show her *real jewels*.

CHAPTER FOUR

- *Ticktock* -

Justin gobbled up the breakfast Grandma had set on the table—pancakes and syrup and apple strudel from an old German recipe. "You're starving!" she exclaimed. "You must have left before the crack of dawn to get out here to the prairie so early on a Sunday morning."

Father laughed. "He woke me up at five o'clock to get started. Couldn't wait to get that little goat and bring her home."

"You've been keeping Ginger, the carriage, and the wagon way down at Thompson's barn because you don't have a real barn for your horse. What will your neighbors say about a goat?" Grandma asked.

"I hope you have a good place to keep her," Grandpa said. "They're so snobby in your neighborhood. Will your neighbors mind having a farm animal on the street?"

"No, they won't mind since we're not selling goat's milk. They'll hardly realize we have a goat there. Justin's built a nice, handy little shed just for her," Father explained. "Charlie helped him. It's a pretty little goat barn that faces away from the wind, and I think she'll be very content in her new home."

"When are you going to build a horse barn for Ginger?" Grandpa asked. "If there was an emergency, you'd be wasting time trying to get your horse hitched up down at Thompson's stables. It's at least a mile from your house."

"I know!" Father said with a touch of irritability in his voice. "There's a lot to do since I've taken over the shop. I do need a barn for Ginger and our carriage, but I just haven't gotten to it yet."

"You have a standard to live up to, son," Grandpa went on. "You've taken over the shop, and I don't mean to sound like a snob, but we've been known as the top jeweler in Chicago. We have a name to live up to."

"We're working on it," Father said. "Charlie said he'd help construct a decent-looking barn for Ginger and our carriage in the spring."

"I don't know what you'd do without Charlie," Grandma said. "He's turning into a fine young man."

And what about me? Justin wondered. *I guess I'm only good for sweeping the floors.*

"What's Charlie been up to?" Grandpa asked.

"He's been helping out at the shop, and what a salesman he's becoming! He's a real asset to the business, let me tell."

Charlie, Charlie, Charlie, Justin thought as he wiped the sticky syrup from his mouth. *Once they get talking about Charlie, they never stop. I know as much about jewels as Charlie—maybe more.*

Charlie was eighteen now, and his future in the family business was always the main topic of conversation. "Let's get my goat into the wagon," Justin suggested.

"Justin's eager to get that little kid," Father said. "That's all we've heard about since you promised her to him."

"She's a sweet little thing, but she's lonely since we sold her mother and sister." Grandma gave Justin a serious look. "You'll have to make up for her loss, Justin."

"I will, Grandma," Justin promised.

"Don't forget—she's a commitment," Grandpa added. "Goats can be a lot of work and expense."

"I'm working for Father now," Justin explained, "so I can pay for feed and stuff like that."

"You're working at the shop?" Grandpa asked with a glance at Justin's father.

"I already know a lot about gemstones. I wish Father would teach me more about the business—like how clocks work and all that," Justin answered. "Then maybe I'd get a chance to do something other than sweep the floors."

"You'll have your day, son," Father said. "It's just that Charlie's older and more capable right now." Then, turning to Grandpa, he added, "He's sure interested in geology and how stones form. In fact, he's been asking me more questions about them today, all the way over here," Father said.

"Hmm." Grandpa grinned. "I thought Justin was more interested in goats!"

"I am!" Justin interrupted. "Let's go get her." He got up and headed for the door.

"Have you decided on a name?" Grandma asked as she followed him.

"Yep. Her name will be Ticktock. Her tail wags like the second hand on a clock."

"There you go." Grandma laughed. "You can tell Justin is the son of a watchmaker."

"I just hope we can talk the little rascal into the wagon," Father said. "This ought to be interesting."

They headed out to the barn. Inside, Ticktock was confined behind a gate that separated her from the other animals. Justin noticed she had a collar on now. He'd use a leash when he took her for a walk.

"Hello, Ticktock." Her little white tail began wagging at Justin's voice.

"She knows her name already," Grandma said. "She's a bright little thing."

"I think she likes you, Justin." Grandpa opened the gate and Ticktock trotted out, her tail wiggling eagerly. She glanced around for a moment and then hurried to Justin's side.

"She most definitely likes you," Grandma agreed.

Justin put out his hand and offered the kid a piece of bread from Grandma's kitchen. The goat's tongue whisked out and grabbed it instantly.

Justin continued offering Ticktock scraps of bread as

they headed toward their wagon. "Come on," he coaxed, holding out his hand. The kid eagerly followed him. "Come on . . . we're going to take you home."

Father set a wide plank from the road up to the bed of the wagon. "Bring her up," he called to Justin. Ginger, the horse, snorted and stamped her hoof. Immediately, Ticktock came to a stop.

"She's scared," Justin said.

"Try chasing her up the ramp," Father said.

"Shoo!" Justin yelled, clapping his hands and stomping his feet behind his new pet. "Shoo! Shoo!"

Instead of running up the ramp, Ticktock gave a jump and ran around to the rear of Justin. Father laughed. "Who's chasing whom here?" he shouted.

"You're scaring her even more by yelling," Grandma warned.

Justin tried running into the wagon and calling her. "Come, Ticktock. Come with me."

But she just bleated and ran around again.

"That goat is too smart," Grandma said. "She's plumb stubborn, too. Look at her tail! It's standing straight up and as still as a pole. No way will she get into that wagon."

Ticktock watched Justin quizzically, her head tilted to one side.

"Aw, she's just afeard of that wagon. She's never been in one," Grandpa said soothingly.

"That's right, Justin. New things can be strange—for goats *and* for people," Grandma said gently. "It'll take a little while, but Ticktock will be fine once she gets used to her new home."

Justin knelt down and put his arms around the kid. "I'll take good care of you, I promise." He rubbed Ticktock's head, where the nubs of her horns had already started to sprout. Ticktock thrust her head against him with a friendly butt.

"Come on." Justin picked up the wiggling bundle. She bleated loudly with all four legs extended in different directions. Justin struggled up the ramp and set her down in the fresh hay they purchased the day before.

"Good! Now she knows who's in charge," Father said.

"Remember, she's a goat," Grandpa added. "Which means she's only letting you *think* you're the boss."

"I'll stay right here with her all the way home," Justin promised.

Justin waved good-bye to his grandparents as his father climbed up onto the driver's seat and clicked the reins. Ticktock folded her legs in the hay and cuddled up next to Justin.

Justin grinned at his new pet. Then he remembered that scruffy girl, Poppy, who had taunted him yesterday: "Goats stink." He put his head down near Ticktock and sniffed. "You're not a bit smelly," he muttered. "Well, maybe it's the smell of hay. That's certainly not a stink."

On Monday, if Poppy really does show up at the shop, I'll have Ticktock with me. He patted his goat's head again.

Father would never let someone like her into the store. But maybe he'd let me show her my geodes—the ones that have the amethyst crystals inside. And the other stones with crystals. She'd be amazed to see that gems really do come from plain old rocks.

"Poppy's just a little girl who doesn't know much about anything," Justin told his goat. "She won't mock me once she sees you and my geodes, Ticktock."

Perhaps I'll get to show her some of the best stones sometime . . . maybe even the big emerald. Once again, he imagined Poppy's eyes widening as he opened the velvet cases filled with sparkling jewels. *She'll know I'm a real expert on gems.*

Before long, the jiggling of the wagon and the sound of Ginger's hooves on the road lulled Justin and his new pet to sleep.

CHAPTER FIVE

- New Girls on the Block -

Sunday night, just when Poppy, Noreen, and Sheila were about to go to bed, Ma Brennan burst into the small room clutching two girls by their shoulders.

"New sisters fer ya!" she roared, shoving both girls onto Poppy's mattress. "You'll share the bed tonight with Poppy. Tomorrow I'll look around for another mattress. You two are gonna start learnin' how to make money—first thing in the mornin'."

Before anyone could ask a question, Ma turned into the hallway and headed up the stairs to the nightclub overhead.

The two strangers parked themselves on Poppy's bed and gawked at their new surroundings. "This place is ugly," said the older one. She looked about fifteen and her brown hair was pulled back and tied with a faded red ribbon.

"I don't want to stay here, Julia," the younger girl whined, her blue eyes filling with tears. "At least the orphanage was clean—and we had beds, not dirty mattresses on the floor."

"Hush up, Renee! You couldn't wait to get away from there. Quit complainin'." Julia turned to Poppy. "I've been takin' care of Renee for 'bout a year now. She gripes a lot."

"You're not sisters, I'm thinkin'," Poppy said, addressing Julia. "I mean, Renee has such blond hair and yours is brown."

"Not even related," Julia answered. "We're both war orphans. Our dads were killed down in Georgia somewhere. Don't even know where they're buried. Renee here was in the half orphanage till her ma died. Then they were goin' to send her to the big home when—"

"That's when I 'scaped," Renee interrupted. "I wasn't goin' to *that* orphanage. I know all about that place. People come pretendin' you're gonna be part of the family, and then all they want is to make you work for them."

Julia agreed with a knowing nod. "Renee would be a slave for the rest of her life."

"What about your mother?" Poppy asked Julia.

"Never knew her. She sent me to my grandma's and I never heard from her again. Grandma yelled a lot, so I ran away."

Wait until she gets slapped a few times by Ma Brennan, Poppy thought. *She won't stay here long, either.*

Sheila came over and squeezed between them on the mattress. "You were smart kids to run away." She peered at Renee's short hair. "How come your hair's so short?"

"She's probably got cooties," Noreen warned. "Don't get close to her."

Sheila jumped away.

"I do not have cooties!" Renee yelled.

"Where do you wash up, then?" Sheila asked.

"In rain barrels," Renee answered.

"And just where do *you* wash up?" Julia snapped. "You three don't look so clean to me. And this place ain't no fancy hotel, either."

"There's a room with real runnin' water down the

hall a little ways—right fresh from the new water tower," Noreen said.

"And it's better than livin' on the streets," said Poppy, hoping to stop the arguing. "Let's go to bed."

"We're gettin' up tomorrow early," Sheila announced. "Ma's givin' these girls a class, and we'll be there to show how it's done."

"I already know how it's done!" Julia kicked off her grimy shoes and plopped her head onto the pillow. "I've been makin' my own way practically since I was borned."

"And Julia taught me how to lift stuff out of stores, so I don't need lessons, either." Renee copied Julia and flipped off her shoes. One flew across the room, landing close to Sheila's bed.

"Watch out, you little street urchin," Sheila bellowed.

"We're all street urchins—including *you*!" Poppy muttered as she curled up on the edge of the mattress. She wished she had the pillow, but since Julia had already put her head on it, Poppy decided she'd do without. After all, she didn't want cooties.

Soon Poppy knew the girls were asleep. Their loud, even breathing resounded in the small, bare room.

Ma came in later, humming a tune, then went to bed. Now the room echoed with her snores.

Poppy couldn't sleep. Instead, she thought about street urchins. The town was full of them, all trying to find a place to live, scrounging around for other folks' leftover food. Poppy had seen the rich people, like the Palmers, who owned many businesses, including the brand-new Palmer House Hotel, in their beautiful clothes and jewels. Why should some people be so rich and others so poor?

Poppy didn't want to grow up and be like Ma Brennan or the ladies that came and went upstairs in the Willow resort. She thought again about her five dollars hidden in the old foundation. Not enough yet to run away.

Tomorrow was Monday. *Isn't that the day that boy, Justin, is going to show me his new goat?* Poppy wondered. *Yes!* He had said he'd be at the jewelry store with his goat after school on Monday.

She chuckled quietly. *How crazy he is . . . bringing a stinking goat to that fancy store! But he wants to show me how his goat makes a good pet—and doesn't stink.* She snickered again. *And he expects me to believe jewels grow out of rocks. He must think I'm stupid to believe that baloney.*

Maybe I'll go see him and his goat tomorrow—if Ma finishes with her lessons by afternoon.

Poppy knew Ma would spend some time teaching the girls how to lift things off store countertops when no one was looking—how to shove them quickly into a sleeve or pocket. Then they'd spend more time nimbly picking one another's pockets—practicing their act of bumping into a mark and causing a scuffle. *You've gotta work on your skills,* Ma always said. And now they'd have to show the new girls.

Yes, Poppy decided. *As soon as Ma's finished, I'll make some excuse and leave. Oh, I hope I get to see Justin and his goat. Maybe I'll even pretend to be his friend. I'm sure he'd show his friend all the beautiful jewels in the shop. Maybe one of those jewels, a good one, would fall into my pocket. Then I could sell it, and I'll run far, far away.*

Poppy put her hands over her ears to drown out Ma's snoring.

CHAPTER SIX

- Randy, Patrick, and Four Fingers Foley -

Early Monday, on the way to school, Justin stopped at his chum Randy's driveway. The two boys usually walked together.

Randy was waiting, standing on his lawn that was yellowed from the drought. "We're early, Justin. Before we go to school, do you want to see the kittens?" Randy asked. "They'll all be gone by Friday, when they'll be six weeks old."

"You got homes for all three of them?"

"Yep. One's going to your sister, Claire, you know.

She's taking it with her when she gets married to Forrest Belmont in December."

"Mother says Claire will need a cat to keep the poor church mice away."

"I'd hate to live in a church," Randy said. "I'd have to be too good."

"Claire won't be living in the church. She'll be next door in the parsonage."

"Still, I wouldn't want to live there. And I wouldn't want to live with Forrest, either, come to think of it. He's so namby-pamby."

"Forrest is a good guy," Justin said. "And he's no sissy."

They walked to a shed in the back of Randy's yard and peeked inside the open door. The mother cat was curled up in a laundry basket with her sleeping babies. Two black and white kittens were snuggled into their mother's fur. The third, who was completely black except for white whiskers, lay off to one side. She yawned and looked up with golden eyes as the boys approached, then put her head between her paws and went back to sleep.

"They sure are cute," Justin whispered. He picked up the black kitten and cuddled it under his chin. "I had the choice of a cat or a goat. I chose the goat—especially once I saw Ticktock at Grandpa's. Besides, a kitten is more of a girl's pet. It'll be fun, though, to have Claire's kitten at our house, too. At least until she moves."

Justin put the kitten back and the two boys walked up to the street. "Whatcha doing this afternoon?" Randy asked. "Going down to State Street?"

"Yes. I'm going to the shop," Justin answered. *Whoops! Randy probably wants to walk with me, and I don't want him around if Poppy shows up. He'd never stop kidding me about meeting a girl.*

"Do you want me to go with you?" Randy asked.

Justin scrambled to think of an excuse. "Not today. I-I'm going to meet someone."

"Whom are you meeting—a customer?"

"Um, yes, sort of."

"What do you mean, 'sort of'? Is your dad letting you sell jewelry?"

Justin frowned. "No, not until I'm older. You know that."

"He lets Charlie sell jewelry. Doesn't he trust you?"

"He'll let me—once I'm Charlie's age."

"So who is this *sort-of customer* you're meeting, then?"

"Don't be so nosy, Randy."

"Well, I don't want to go anyway. It's too warm already. It'll be really hot this afternoon." Randy took a handkerchief from his back pocket and wiped the sweat off his forehead.

The sound of bells and horses' hooves seemed close by. The boys looked around and could see fire trucks down the street, where a stream of black smoke spiraled to the blue sky.

"I nearly got run over by one of those fire engines yesterday." Randy wiped his forehead again.

"That'll teach you not to walk in the street," Justin said.

"I don't envy those firemen, working with those big steamers on the trucks. They must be sweating down to their bones, standing there for hours, shooting water from those heavy hoses."

Suddenly two boys jumped out at them from behind a fence. The bigger of the two, Patrick Cahill, was dressed in rough stained overalls and a raggedy plaid shirt. "Well, if it ain't the fancy-pants kids from the Rotten Academy," he said, dragging out the word "academy" in a singsong voice. The *real* name of Justin's private school was Rodham

Academy, but the tough kids from Conley's Patch, who hadn't attended any school for years, had their own name for it: Rotten Academy.

Patrick's pal, who stood nearby with a sneering grin, was called Four Fingers Foley because he had lost one of his fingers when his hand had got stuck in a warehouse door. Most everyone just called him Fingers. "Why, it's Justin and Randall, the bigwig boys from the big-shot school," Fingers taunted. "What are ya goin' to learn today? How to make a million bucks sellin' pretty jewels to the rich ladies?"

"We're learning to ignore the mudsills of society," Randy said.

"Shh! Don't ask for trouble," Justin whispered as he pulled his friend by the arm toward the entrance to the school.

"Go on home—your mother's calling ya," Randy sang out over his shoulder. "Your father just fell in a garbage can. Go on home—your mother's callin' ya. They've come to collect your old man!"

"Aw, shut up, Randy." Justin slammed his hand over Randy's mouth. "You're just baiting them."

"Don't you say anything about my old man!" Fingers

started after them again. But the boys were almost to the double doors of the school.

"That's it—run away, like rats," Patrick howled. "Next time we'll beat you up!"

"Yeah! I'm not forgettin' what you just said about my old man," Fingers added.

"I sure hope we never see them again," Justin said. "They're probably already thinking of ways to beat us up or rob our shop."

"Nah. They're just a lot of talk," Randy said as he pulled open the door and went into the large oak-paneled hallway. "Are you going to the shop after school? Or are you going home to change clothes first? I suppose you have to dress up when you go into your dad's fancy place down State Street."

"Of course. My father expects me to look decent at the shop. After all, Butterworth's is the best jewelry store in Chicago—and my father is the best watchmaker," Justin said. "I'll go home and change into better clothes. So meet me after school. We'll walk home together—just in case Fingers and Patrick show up."

The walk home after school was uneventful, but nevertheless, Justin and Randy walked close together and avoided the area where Fingers and Patrick had darted out from behind the fence.

Once Justin got home and changed his clothes, he hitched his goat to a leash and petted her. Ticktock rubbed her head against Justin's hand and butted him gently. "Come on—let's go down to the shop, just in case that Poppy shows up. I'll show her what a good pet you are. And we'll prove that goats don't stink."

He paused, thinking. Then he quickly raced into the house and returned with a bottle of his father's best shaving lotion.

"Here you go, Ticktock," he said, rubbing the lotion over the goat's head and neck. "A little help in the smell department won't hurt."

CHAPTER SEVEN

- Ma Brennan's School for Girls -

It was hard to tell when dawn came, as the cellar holes where Poppy lived were so deep that the rooms were gloomy and dark all day, even when it was bright and sunny outside.

Poppy lay still, cramped onto a small section of mattress, and her neck felt stiff, but she didn't dare pull the pillow out from under Julia's head. The thought of cooties horrified her. She remembered the time she and Ma's girls had cooties and how Ma had washed their hair in kerosene oil. Sometimes when their hair needed washing now, the smell of kerosene still lingered. Poppy wondered what would happen if she got too close to a kerosene lantern with that stuff in her hair. Would her hair catch on fire? She pushed the thought out of her mind.

Ma snorted a long grunt, then slowly sat up in bed. "Get up, girls. School today. Be out in the kitchen for breakfast in five minutes." She pulled on a faded house-dress over her nightgown and stumbled out into the kitchen across the hall.

Breakfast was toast with jelly and tea. Renee and Julia picked at the toast, complaining that they wanted bacon or oatmeal. "You'd think you were brought up in Buckingham Palace, instead of being low-down street kids," Sheila said with a sniff.

Poppy couldn't help laughing. "And we aren't street people?"

"No, we're not!" Noreen snapped. "We have a nice home here with Ma."

Ma turned on her heel and glared at Poppy. "You're nothin' but an ungrateful guttersnipe. Don't forget for one minute that's where I found you—in the gutter. Your own mother didn't want you."

Poppy could put up with Ma and the girls calling

her ugly names. But whenever Ma reminded her that she was a foundling—that her own mother had thrown her away—it wounded Poppy to the pit of her stomach. She could feel hot tears rising and turned away quickly before they slipped down—before Ma and the girls could see them.

"Finish up, and let's practice your skills," Ma said, leading them down the hall to a large, windowless room. Ma lit an overhead lantern near a big pool table in the center of the room. "Let's pretend this table is a store counter. I'll put things on here, and I want to see how well you lift the stuff—and see where you hide it." She gestured to a pile of bags and purses, jackets, and clothes that were too large for any of the girls. They all put on garments that had large pockets inside and outside.

Ma spread purses and various kinds of junk jewelry around the edge of the table. "I'll demonstrate first." She stood back, arms crossed, as she sauntered around the room, then casually slid up to the table, pretending to examine the purses and paraphernalia. Over the span of several minutes, Ma skillfully and silently slipped a few pieces of jewelry and a small purse into her coat and pockets. "See how easy it is? Now it's your turn. My girls will go first. Go ahead, Sheila. Show the new girls how it's done."

"We already know how it's done," Julia grumbled.

Ma slapped Julia's back. "Shut up and watch!"

"No one does it better than me," Sheila said as she wandered around the room, as if she were in a store. Then little by little she made her way to the "counter," pretending to show an interest in the jewelry. She picked up one sparkly brooch, turned it over, and was about to set it down when she "accidentally" knocked it to the floor. She quickly put her foot over it. After looking around, she bent over, picked it up, and shoved it into the hidden pocket in her coat.

"That was pretty good, Sheila," said Ma. "But you could have moved your foot over the piece quicker."

Sheila's mouth drooped angrily. "But, Ma . . ."

Ma ignored her. "Your turn, Noreen. You show how much better you are."

Noreen had her turn, this time stealing a bulky purse from the counter and shoving it into an inside pocket.

"No!" Ma screamed. "Don't pick the biggest purse. You can see that huge bump in your coat. Can't you see how risky it would be?"

Poppy watched as Noreen's face reddened. "What did you put it out there on the table for, then?" Noreen yelled.

"To see if you'd be stupid enough to steal it!" Ma yelled back. She took a deep breath. "Your turn, Poppy. I hope you can show Julia and Renee that you've learned something here. My own daughters are a disgrace!"

Julia and Renee giggled behind their hands while Noreen and Sheila fumed. Poppy began her walk around the pretend store, stopping here and there to look at various objects on the counter. After examining a dozen or more items, she walked away.

"What are you doing?" Ma asked. "Go back and take one of the things I put on the table!"

Poppy reached into the cuff of her coat and displayed a shiny silver bracelet.

"Oh! That was slick!" Julia said admiringly.

Poppy reached into the cuff of the other sleeve and brought out a jeweled ring.

Ma, Julia, Renee, and Sheila clapped their hands, while Noreen turned away, pouting.

Poppy grinned. "Biggest isn't always best." She held up the ring. "Small things are easier to steal, and a real piece like this could be worth a lot more than a big purse that might be empty." She reached into her pocket and pulled out a square of wax in a small matchbox.

"Now, just look at that," Ma said. "Poppy never forgets her wax. She's always prepared for anything that might come up—like makin' an impression of a key. Which of you girls still have the wax I gave you?" Ma waited, but Sheila and Noreen dropped their gazes to the floor and didn't answer. "See? Poppy gives me more trouble than any of you, but she's my star pupil." Ma grinned. "So, Poppy wins the prize."

"A prize?" Sheila exclaimed. "You didn't tell us we'd get a prize."

Noreen stomped her foot. "Ma! You always treat Poppy better than you treat us."

Humph, thought Poppy. *Since when?*

"She always does better than you—my *real* daughters. Poppy gets what she deserves all the time—and that includes a slap now and then when it's necessary." Ma turned to Julia and Renee and pointed to Noreen and Sheila. "Just because these two are my flesh and blood doesn't mean I play favorites. Poppy was best today, so she gets the prize." She pulled a bag of candy from her pocket and handed it to Poppy. "Here you go, Poppy. And never say I'm not fair."

Poppy offered candy to everyone, but Noreen wouldn't take any. Instead, she turned away and faced the wall when Poppy held out the bag to her. "Ma thinks you're so smart, Poppy. And you're *so cute*. Once again, you get the prize."

"Don't get yourself into a pucker, Noreen," Poppy said. "It's only a bag of candy."

"Enough, girls. Time to get out there and bring home the sugar," Ma said. "I have new rules. Each of you must find five hits today. If you do, you'll have a chance at another prize."

"Five hits!" Julia exclaimed. "That'll take all day and we'll end up in the cooler!"

"Not if you do it right," Ma argued. "Poppy, you can do some work at the bank counters with Sheila. Here's a couple of ten-dollar bills. *I want these back when you come home.*" She gave both girls a warning look as she handed the money to Sheila. "You two know the game—you've done well with it before."

"We can't do five hits apiece, then. It's too danger-ous," Sheila argued. "The banks will be searchin' for us."

"Right you are. Five between ya both," Ma agreed. "Now, Noreen, you can work one at a time with Julia and Renee. Take a few stores and try what you've learned today. It will be good practice for them. Renee ought to be able to get some sympathy just sittin' on the sidewalk and cryin' that she's hungry. Folks will toss her a few coins just to keep her quiet, if not out of pity." She led the five girls into the hall and up the steps to the outside. "Off with ya, now. Get back before dark. I worry when you're late."

"Yeah, she worries, all right," Poppy whispered to Julia. "She worries that she's missin' out on money. She never worries about *us*."

Several banks had businesses down by the Chicago River. Sheila and Poppy chose one that was on a side street. They casually glanced into the foyer, where several businessmen were counting money from checks they had cashed. "Wait until there's just one man there," Sheila whispered. "Once we're inside, you be the one to drop the money." She slipped the ten-dollar bills into Poppy's dress pocket.

The girls walked up the street so as not to bring attention to themselves. When they returned, one man was left at the counting table, where he had placed money in neat piles of ones, fives, tens, and twenty-dollar bills.

Sheila walked into the bank and up to the next table, taking out one of the withdrawal forms. Sheila had taught herself how to write a little. As she pretended to be making out the form, Poppy entered the bank and looked around, as if she were deciding where she should go.

Then, as if she had changed her mind, she headed back toward the front door by way of the counting table. As she passed, she let Ma's ten-dollar bills fall to the floor unnoticed.

"Oh, my goodness," she said innocently. "Did you drop that money?" She pointed to the ten-dollar bills on the floor and looked at the man at the counting table.

"I must have," he said, bending over to pick them up. "Thank you."

While he was retrieving the bills, quick as a blink, Sheila grabbed a handful of the twenty-dollar bills, stuffed them into her shirt, and walked swiftly out the door. Poppy was already outside and racing for a back alley up the street.

Before the businessman realized he'd been robbed, both Poppy and Sheila would have disappeared.

"How much did you get?" Poppy asked as Sheila counted six crisp new bills.

"Twenty, forty, sixty, eighty, one hundred. What comes after that?"

"I dunno," Poppy answered. "After a hundred, I think you start countin' again."

"I'll start over. Twenty, forty, sixty, eighty, one hundred, twenty dollars! Holy cow—Ma isn't going to believe her eyes. That was a real good haul, Poppy."

"But you don't have Ma's two ten-dollar bills anymore."

"No, but we have all this!"

Poppy often lived in fear of Ma's wrath. "Ma said she wanted them back."

Sheila rolled her eyes. "Why don't you go and ask the man to give them back to you, you dumbbell."

"I guess you're right," Poppy said, feeling stupid.

CHAPTER EIGHT

- Ticktock Goes to Town -

All the way to State Street, people stopped and grinned to see Justin with his little goat in tow. "Cute little kid," was the usual comment. Folks reached out to pet her, and when they did, Ticktock's tongue flicked out much like a snake's, hoping for something to eat. She never pulled against the leash but stayed close by Justin, her little legs trotting at a fast pace to keep up with him while her short tail wagged like a flag.

When they arrived at the shop, Justin remembered Father's warning: "Don't bring that goat into the front of the store. It wouldn't be proper, and other shopkeepers will complain to have a farm animal tethered on the front steps." So Justin took his pet to the courtyard out back where Ticktock could nibble on a grassy plot, although the grass was dry and yellow from the drought. Ticktock seemed content, and Justin knocked at the back door, which was always locked.

"Who's there?" It was Father's voice.

"It's me. I came down for a walk and brought Ticktock with me."

Father unlocked and opened the door. "Come in, Justin. I'm busy right now. I'm about to set the big emerald into this white-gold pendant for Mrs. Palmer. She'll be coming to approve it soon." He held the necklace up to the back window, where it picked up the sunlight and cast rainbows on the wall. Then he placed the jewelry and chain into Justin's hand. "The stone isn't set in permanently yet. Once she approves it, I'll set the prongs and do a little more soldering."

Justin held the lacy pendant in his hand. The gold prongs that would firmly clasp the emerald were formed into tiny leaves and flowers. "Oh, Father! If this don't beat all," Justin whispered in awe. "It's the most beautiful thing in the world. I'd say the best you've ever done!"

"I'm glad you think so, son. I hope Mrs. Palmer does, too." His father took the piece back, rubbed it with a soft cloth, and then deposited it into his pocket.

"She will. I'd reckon no one in the whole city of Chicago ever saw anything as handsome as that."

Charlie appeared from the sales room, where they displayed all the jewelry. "I'd sure love to try my hand at setting a valuable stone."

"There's a nice topaz in the safe. Why don't you give it a try? I think you've got just the artistic flair to be a great jeweler, Charlie." Father clapped his hand on Charlie's shoulder as the two men went back to the office, leaving Justin by himself.

Humph! Charlie—the artist! No wonder he's so good—Father gives him every chance to try new things. All I get to do is sweep the sidewalk.

Oh, well, perhaps I should go out on the sidewalk and sweep, Justin thought with a resigned sigh. *That way I'll be able to spot Poppy if she shows up.* He pulled the broom and dustpan from the closet, then went to the front entry.

"Good idea, Justin," Father said when he saw Justin head out the door with the gear. "The way the dust is blowing, the whole city will be knee-deep in dirt before long."

"We sure need rain," Charlie commented.

Once outside, Justin began sweeping. The wind had again blown the dust into ridges of dirt, the way the lake left creases in the sand as it lapped against the shore.

He had just finished the entry and was moving out to the sidewalk when he saw Poppy skipping up the wooden walkway like an eight- or nine-year-old. *How come she dresses like a little kid?* he wondered. *Perhaps she can't be picky. Her clothes are probably hand-me-downs, and since she's so small anyway, she looks younger than she really is.*

Justin knew by the way Poppy spoke—with a tough and angry tone—that she was one of the street kids. She was probably from Conley's Patch, the toughest neighborhood around. It was easy to spot those rowdies with their out-of-style old clothes and surly manners, especially on State Street, where everyone else was well dressed and mannerly.

"Well, well, look who the cat dragged in," Poppy called out as she came to a clattering stop, dust blowing up around her legs. "I don't see any goat here today. I'm bettin' you don't have one after all."

"Ticktock's out back. Come with me and I'll show you." Justin set the broom down and motioned for Poppy to step inside.

"Yeah, and I want to see those rocks with jewels growin' out of 'em, too."

"We'll go out this way," Justin told her, leading her through the store to the back room. Poppy followed him, her eyes taking in the glass showcases. "It's beautiful in here," she whispered as she paused to gape at the sparkling jewels and watches.

Charlie came out of the office and stopped in his tracks when he saw Poppy. "Who is *this*?"

"Um, this is Poppy, Charlie," Justin answered awkwardly. "She just came to see Ticktock."

"Well, don't bring her through the store!" Charlie said. "Take her out and around to the back."

Justin grabbed Poppy's arm and was about to go through the front door when the bells jingled and a tall, well-dressed woman in a large hat stepped inside. She looked at Poppy quizzically and then at Justin.

"Good morning, Mrs. Palmer," Charlie was saying graciously. "My father has been working on your beautiful pendant. I'll go get him."

But Father had heard the door and came out from his office. He looked surprised when he saw Poppy and whispered with an undertone, "Uh, Justin, bring this . . . this child out back, please." He propelled Justin and Poppy into the back room and shut the door.

Justin could hear his father's warm exclamation to his well-paying customer. "Oh, Mrs. Palmer, let me show you the setting I've chosen for the pendant. You will be absolutely thrilled, I promise."

Justin jostled Poppy through the back room. "Why'd your dad show me the exit?" Poppy demanded. "I ain't seen those rocks you promised to show me—the ones that grow jewels."

Justin peeked into the sales room, where both his father and Charlie were busy showing Mrs. Palmer the necklace.

"Quick, come here." Justin took Poppy's hand and pulled her toward the window, where his geode collection was set on the sill. He picked a round rock that had been sawed in two, then opened the top. "Look what's inside." He handed the bottom half of the stone to Poppy.

"Oh my stars and garters!" Poppy exclaimed. "Look at all them purple jewels. They *are* growin' out of the rock!"

Justin nodded. "Just as I told you. Those crystals are amethysts."

"Are you takin' them out of the rock to make jewelry?"

"No, they're not perfect stones. I collect geodes just for fun." Justin looked around and could see that his father was still with Charlie and Mrs. Palmer. The door to his father's office was open, as was the safe. "Stay here," he said to Poppy. Then he slipped into the office and pulled a big velvet bag out of the safe.

"If you think those amethysts are pretty, then take a look at this." He opened the bag by the back window and let the jewels trickle through his fingers in the sunlight.

The sunbeams burst in a dozen rainbows as they touched the diamonds, topaz, and a huge ruby.

Poppy gasped and put her hand to her mouth. "Oh! I ain't never in all my borned days seen anything so gorgeous. They're like somethin' you'd see in a queen's crown . . . or in a fairy tale. I can't ever believe anything so beautiful could come out of the dirty ground."

"Well, they usually have to be cut and polished when they're first mined. But they really do come out of mines deep in the earth." Justin pulled the cord that closed the bag and shoved it back into the safe in the office. "You ought to see the emerald Father's showing Mrs. Palmer. It's as big as an egg." He glanced toward the door to the sales room again. "You've got to leave, Poppy, before I get in trouble."

"All right, I'm leavin'." Poppy followed Justin to the back door.

Justin unlocked the door to the courtyard with the key that his father had left in the lock. "That's Father's most important customer in there," he said as he opened the door and shoved Poppy outside. "It's *the* Mrs. Palmer—you know, the high-society lady."

"You mean the rich Mrs. Palmer what owns the big hotel?"

"That's the one." Justin headed over to Ticktock, who was curled up on the dry grass with her head tucked down and eyes closed. "Here's my goat." He looked over to Poppy, but she was just standing there, looking down at her feet. One shoe was missing.

"Oh, dear. When your dad pushed us, he knocked off my shoe. I'm goin' back for it." She headed for the door that led into the back room.

"No, you can't go in there again. Father will get mad."

"I need my shoe." Before Justin could grab her, Poppy had opened the door and slipped into the back room.

"Come out of there, Poppy!" Justin ran after her, but she had already retrieved her shoe and was sitting on the step, pulling it on.

Charlie opened the door. "Who was just in the store?"

"Poppy left her shoe inside," Justin answered.

"Go on home, Justin. And take the goat with you," Charlie called as he closed the door. "And send Poppy home, please."

"I know when I'm not wanted," Poppy said, her nose in the air. "I'm leavin' right now."

MONDAY EVENING,
OCTOBER 2, 1871

CHAPTER NINE

- *Poppy's Nice-Girl Dress* -

Poppy patted the pocket on her old pinafore dress where she had slipped the matchbox of wax. How smart she'd been to leave her shoe inside the jewelry shop—a perfect excuse to go back, remove the key from inside the back door, and make a quick impression in the wax. She was as fast as greased lightning and replaced the key before anyone even knew she'd touched it.

Justin's father treated me like dirt, sending me away from his highfalutin store. Well, he'll be sorry when I get inside and help myself to whatever I want—like those sparkly jewels. I felt like I was in a dream when I saw them, 'cept they were real. Maybe those jewels are magical and they can get me away from Chicago! And I'll never have to steal anything again.

She grinned. *Ma would be proud of me if she knew I have an impression for a key to that shop. But I'll never let her know. She'd keep it all and I'd end up with a bag of penny candy.*

"Poppy! Poppy!" Justin called after her. "Are you listening?"

"What?" she answered crossly, coming to a stop.

"I asked you if you'd like to go to my house. My sister, Claire, made pastries today." Justin glanced at Poppy. "So do you want to come? It's not too far. Just a couple of miles."

Poppy shrugged. "I guess so. She'll probably throw me out, too."

"She won't. Come on." He had leashed his goat and was heading for the street. "I hope you're not scared of my father."

Poppy followed along in a grumpy pout. "I ain't a-scared of anyone." She stopped and looked Justin straight in the eye. "Your dad don't want me in his store 'cause I'm a street girl from Conley's Patch. Right?"

Justin turned away from her gaze. "Well, he does have real important people coming to his shop."

A woman stopped to pet Ticktock and asked her name.

"Ticktock—like a clock," Justin answered. "My dad's the watchmaker and jeweler on State Street."

"I know that place. I've heard your father is an excellent jeweler and watchmaker," the woman commented. "And I remember your grandfather, too, when he ran the shop. I hear he's retired and moved out to the prairie." She patted Ticktock again. "What a delightful little kid—and what a charming name for your goat." The woman waved good-bye.

How come people treat Justin—and even his goat—better than they treat me? Poppy wondered as they started walking again. She glanced at her faded, worn dress with a hole under the arm. *Everyone can tell I'm a nobody. Even my mother didn't want me.* Poppy kicked a stone off the wooden sidewalk. *And here I am, going off to Justin's house. His sister will probably go plumb crazy when she sees me tagging along.*

Still, Justin showed me the jewels. I don't think he'd do that for everybody. I think he likes me—kind of.

Poppy suddenly felt sad. Here she had made a wax of the key so she could return and rob the store. *Justin would be mad if he ever found out . . . and he wouldn't like me anymore.*

They hadn't talked much during the long walk and

already they were turning onto a driveway. Justin pointed out his house. "It's this white one. We'll take Ticktock to the side where I keep her, and then I'll bring you inside to meet my sister and my mother, too."

They walked up the driveway and into the side yard.

"I'm not goin' in," said Poppy. "I'll wait outside with your goat."

Justin ignored her as he unlatched the gate into the goat's pen. "Take a look at Ticktock's shed. My father and Charlie helped me build it." He unleashed his goat, who ran to a pail of water next to the shack.

Poppy took in a quick breath when she saw the neat red and white shed. It even had a window and a real door! She peeked inside to see a pile of fresh hay and a quilt folded on a shelf. A bucket with brushes was on another shelf. "I ain't never seen a goat house before. I'm thinkin' that goats have it better than some people."

Justin took out a large brush from the bucket inside the shed and began brushing Ticktock's bristly coat. The goat rubbed against the brush, then nudged Justin gently with her head. When he had finished, Justin stood and crossed his arms on his chest. "So what do you think about goats for pets now that you've seen my kid?"

Poppy had to agree that Ticktock was rather sweet, the way she trotted alongside Justin. "I'll allow that goats do make good pets—and pretty lucky ones, too, to have a house of their own and someone to care for them." She watched as Ticktock looked up at Justin, watching his every move and following him wherever he went. "She likes you a lot."

"Yep, she does." Justin bent down and hugged the goat. "You're my good girl, aren't you, Ticktock?" The goat nuzzled Justin's face and neck and nibbled on his hair. Justin laughed and pushed her away.

Poppy couldn't help laughing, too. "I heard goats eat anything. Looks like she wants to eat you!"

"Justin!" someone called from the house. "Are you coming in? Are we going to meet your friend?"

"It's my sister, Claire. She always wants me to introduce new friends."

Poppy cringed at the word "introduce." What did he mean? What should she do? Shake hands? Curtsy? No one had taught her how to be introduced. "No, I've got to go home," she said.

Claire came down the front steps of the house and walked to the pen. "Hello," she said, putting out her hand. "I'm Justin's sister, Claire. What is your name, dear?"

"I'm Poppy," Poppy replied, taking Claire's hand.

"Poppy . . . ?" Claire waited for Poppy's last name.

"Um. Brennan."

"Won't you come in?" Claire asked. "Justin knows I made pastries for a church fair this weekend—and there's plenty to spare."

Poppy allowed herself to be coaxed inside to a large, round oak table in the center of the kitchen. Another woman was stirring what smelled like chicken soup on the stove.

"This is our mother, Mrs. Butterworth," Claire said. "Mother, this is Justin's friend, Poppy Brennan. She came to visit."

Mrs. Butterworth took a quick look at Poppy from head to foot, and Poppy was sickeningly aware of her soiled dress and pinafore, the rip under her armpit, and the shoes that didn't quite match.

"Please excuse my appearance, Mrs. Butterworth," Poppy said. "All my clothes are at the laundry." She smiled, showing her teeth as Ma Brennan had taught her. *That smile will charm anyone,* Ma always said.

"Oh, I see." Mrs. Butterworth and Claire exchanged glances. "Perhaps Claire can help you out. You have some things that you've outgrown that might fit Poppy, don't you? Since her clothes are all at the laundry?"

"Why, yes, I do, as a matter of fact. There's a sweet dress that might just fit you."

Poppy couldn't speak. *A dress? For me?*

"Come with me, dear," Claire said, taking Poppy's hand. "I think you'd look wonderful in that dress." She guided Poppy out of the kitchen and into the hall.

Mrs. Butterworth said, "While you try the dress, I'll set out some of Claire's pastries."

Poppy followed Claire to a bedroom off the hall. Poppy stood in awe at the shiny brass bed, covered with a pure white spread. The late afternoon sun glistened through the windowpanes, casting a mellow light on a hand-braided rug. On the windowsill were several rocks.

"You collect jewel rocks too?" Poppy asked.

"Yes, I have a small collection. I love to see the shiny sparklers tucked inside." Claire took a rock from the sill and handed it to Poppy. "See this gem?" She pointed to a dark green crystal that was part of the rock. "This is tourmaline. It came from Maine."

Poppy held the stone in the sunlight. "There's a green rainbow inside."

"Yes. It collects the sunbeams and shines them back in pretty colors," Claire said as she set the rock back on her windowsill.

Claire then opened a maple chest at the foot of her bed and pulled out a forest green dress made of some soft, warm material. The collar and sleeves were trimmed with a heavy crocheted lace. "This was a dress my grandmother made for me, when I was about your size. I always loved it." Claire held the dress up to Poppy. "Oh, yes, this will fit, I'm sure."

Poppy's hands shook as she touched the downy fabric. "This is right . . . grand." Was she supposed to pay for the dress? Or were they *giving* it to her? Why? They didn't even know her.

"Take off your pinafore, and then I'll help you with your dress," Claire said.

Poppy undid the pinafore and felt the box of wax, which was still deep in the pocket. She put the pinafore carefully on the bed so the box would not fall out.

Claire undid the few buttons that closed the back of Poppy's bodice, and her unsightly dress dropped to the floor. As Poppy stepped out of it, Claire picked it up warily and tossed it aside. Then she slipped the green gown over Poppy's head, buttoned the back, and straightened the skirt. "Oh, Poppy! It's a perfect fit. And to think I was about to send it down to the church fair tomorrow."

Poppy turned to look in the tall mirror that stood by the bureau, but Claire pulled her away. "No, don't look at yourself yet." Claire took a wide-toothed ivory comb and a green ribbon from the dresser drawer, and after combing Poppy's hair until it was smooth over her shoulders, she tied it back with the ribbon. "Now see yourself in the mirror, Poppy. You look lovely!"

The girl in the mirror was a stranger—a pretty, *good-girl* kind of stranger. Not Poppy, the pickpocket. Suddenly Poppy swung around. "Are you giving me this dress?"

"Of course!"

"Why?" Poppy demanded. "Is this a trick?"

"Why would I trick you?"

"You just now met me and you're giving me this dress. There's got to be a catch to it somewhere," she said accusingly. She ripped the ribbon from her hair and tossed it onto the bed.

"I'm sorry you feel that way," Claire said. "Take the dress off and I'll put it away with the other things for the fair."

Poppy looked at her image in the mirror again. *A nice dress doesn't make me a nice girl, does it? I'm still Poppy, the pickpocket.*

Suddenly she felt tears filling her eyes and overflowing down her cheeks. "Don't you understand?" she whimpered. "You don't even know me."

"Don't cry, Poppy. I'm sorry I upset you. And you're right. We just met and this is probably overwhelming." Claire put her arms around Poppy. "There, there. Don't cry."

Poppy dropped her head onto Claire's shoulder until her tears and sobs were finished.

CHAPTER TEN

- *Trouble Brewing* -

Justin helped himself to another pastry. What was keeping his sister and Poppy? All she was going to do was try on a dress. *Claire will be the perfect parson's wife,* Justin thought. Once she'd seen how needy Poppy was, she'd just had to come to the rescue. Still, Poppy sure could use some decent clothes.

The front door opened and Charlie strode in. "I had a busy day at the shop," he said as he put his hat and jacket on the hook by the door. "I'm plumb tuckered out."

"Your father is so proud of you," Mother said. "You're a boon to the business."

Oh, here we go again, Justin thought with a sullen frown. *Charlie's a boon to the business.*

Mother took a coffeepot off the stove and peeked inside. "There's another cup of coffee in here, Charlie. Why don't you have it with one of Claire's pastries? Supper won't be ready until your father gets home."

"Where is Father?" Justin asked, hoping Poppy would leave before his father arrived.

"He's working on the books. He should be home soon." Charlie sat at the table and helped himself to a pastry.

At that moment Claire and Poppy came into the kitchen. "Here she is in her new dress," Claire said, gesturing to Poppy, who walked in slowly, looking at the floor. "Fits her perfectly!"

"Oh, you look charming, Poppy," Mother said as she handed the cup of coffee to Charlie.

"Thank you," Poppy said softly. "I ain't never had a dress as nice as this."

Charlie was about to take a bite of his pastry when he stopped, looking puzzled. "Is this the girl who was at the store today?"

"Yes," Justin replied. "She's the one."

Charlie was silent for a moment, and then he shrugged and commenced eating.

"I wouldn't have recognized you, either, had I met you downtown," Justin said to Poppy. She was actually pretty with her coffee-colored hair pulled back with a ribbon, instead of hiding her face in unkempt strands.

"It's getting late," Claire noted. "Won't your family be worried, Poppy?"

"No, ma'am," Poppy said. "No one will miss me."

"Where do you live?" Charlie asked.

Poppy looked down at her hands, which she was clasping and unclasping. "Up on Wells Street, near Clark."

No one spoke. Everyone knew that section of town was where Conley's Patch was located—a dangerous place to be, especially at night.

Mother began dishing chicken stew into a bowl. "Poppy, eat this soup now. And then head home full chisel. I think you can make it before dark." She placed the soup, a spoon, and a large chunk of still-warm fresh bread in front of Poppy and made her sit down.

Claire tucked a napkin into the neck of Poppy's dress. "Here you go, love. Eat up. I think you could use a good meal."

Poppy glanced around, then began to eat, dipping the spoon and slurping the soup without a pause. When she finished, she looked up at Justin's mother. "It's right good, ma'am. The best soup I ever ate in my whole borned days." She wiped her mouth with the napkin and then got up. "I'd better go."

Claire handed Poppy a satchel. "Here are your other clothes, Poppy."

Poppy took the bag and headed for the door. "Bye, Justin. I do like your goat."

"I'll walk some of the way with you," Justin said, looking to his mother for permission.

"Just up to the next block," Mother said, opening the front door. "And get back for supper."

Justin and Poppy walked down the street together, not saying much. "I'll go a little farther with you and then I have to go back," he told her.

"You can go back now. I'll be okay. No one's goin' to hurt me. I'm Ma Brennan's girl, and she'd fix any varmint who laid a hand on me."

"Well, that's excellent," Justin replied. "She takes good care of you, then."

"But she's not like *your* mother," Poppy said. "Your

mother talks nice, and I'll bet she never clobbers you."

"Of course not. Does Ma Brennan clobber you?"

"All the time."

They crossed onto Wells Street and stopped. "Uh-oh. You'd better go home now," said Poppy. "I see trouble ahead." She gestured to two boys up the street who were looking their way. "That's Four Fingers Foley and Patrick Cahill."

Justin turned to go back. "I'm getting out of here before they see me."

"Hey! Rotten!" yelled Patrick. "You just wait a second." He started running toward Justin and Poppy, with Four Fingers close behind him.

Sure, they come after me when I'm alone with a girl, Justin thought. He was about to turn and run but then stopped. What would happen to Poppy if he left her? *That would be a dishonorable thing to do,* he thought.

"Scram, Justin!" Poppy yelled. "They'll make mincemeat out of you."

"I'm not leaving you with those guys, Poppy."

"I don't think they'll hurt me. Run! Run, Justin."

But Justin had hesitated too long. The two rowdies were already on him, cuffing and punching.

"Get off me! Leave me alone! Leave Poppy alone!" Justin fought back, kicking and swinging, while Poppy clouted the two boys with her satchel.

"Get away from him!" she yelled. "I'll get Roger Plant's kids after ya! You know who I mean. He owns the Willow, where I live!"

At the mention of Roger Plant, the two boys immediately stopped their attack on Justin. "Well, well, you've got a little girl to save ya," said Fingers. "Ain't you the brave one."

"Next time we'll get you when you're alone," Patrick promised.

"Why? What did I ever do to you?" Justin brushed off his suit and retrieved his cap. His eye was swollen and his belly hurt where Fingers had slugged him.

"What did I ever do to you?" mimicked Patrick in a whining voice. "You just *are*. That's enough."

"I'm telling Mr. Plant on you. He'll fix you good," Poppy yelled, giving Fingers a final swat with her satchel. "Now get out of here."

The two boys skulked away. "We'll be watchin' for you," said Fingers. "And you, too, *Poppy*."

"My knees are knockin', I'm so a-scared," Poppy taunted.

The boys disappeared into the shadows of an alley.

"Go on home, Justin. I'll be all right."

"Looks like you will," Justin agreed. "You settled their hash just fine. That name you flung around scared 'em off good."

"I live here, and I know the ropes," Poppy said. "Mr. Plant is the big boss of Conley's Patch."

"I feel sorry for you, living around people like that," Justin said.

"Nah, don't feel sorry for me," Poppy said. "I can take care of myself."

She nodded to him and headed down the wooden planks that made up the sidewalk.

CHAPTER ELEVEN

- Nowhere to Go -

The sound of Poppy's footsteps clattered on the planks. Where were those two boys—Fingers and Patrick—who'd taunted Justin? She hoped she wouldn't run into them again.

The satchel she carried swung from her arm, and she suddenly remembered the new dress she wore, the one Justin's sister had given her.

Why was Claire so nice to me? She don't even know me. Yet here she gave me this pretty dress and brushed my hair—as if I were part of their family or someone like them—and she never said a bad word to me. And when I cried and told how I wasn't a real good girl, she said she loved me. She showed me that rock—the one with the green crystal. What was it she said? "You're like this stone, Poppy—deep inside, there's a sparkling crystal of goodness."

Poppy felt warm whenever she thought of Claire and the things she had said. Even the rest of the family had been nice to her, too. Mrs. Butterworth had given her soup and had said she was charming.

Her heart raced and she was breathless as she ran toward the Willow. Across the street was the empty lot where she had hidden her five dollars. Suddenly she stopped, remembering the wax impression of the key to the Butterworths' jewelry store. She had planned to have a key made so she could steal something from the shop and run away.

How would Claire and her mother and Justin feel if they knew Poppy had robbed their store?

What should she do? She needed to think about it. But first she'd hide the key impression—for now, anyway.

It was hard to find the gray rock in the wall where she'd hidden her money. All the stones—even her sparkly one—looked alike in this light, so she tried jiggling several until she came upon one that almost fell into her hand as she wiggled it. Reaching into the cavity, she pulled out the can where she had secreted the money.

She tipped the can upside down and the bills fell out into her palm. The money was still there, just as she had left it! She reached into the satchel, where she had placed her old clothes. The small matchbox was still tucked inside the pocket of her pinafore. She removed the box carefully—if it bent, it would ruin the impression of the key. Then she inserted the box into the can, put back the bills, slipped the can into the hole, and replaced the stone.

I don't have to do anything yet, she decided. *I'll make up my mind later what I'll do with the key.*

It was darker now, and she stumbled over rocks and junk until she got onto the street again. Lantern lights glistened in the windows of the Willow just ahead. The girls were probably home by now, and Ma might be mad that Poppy was returning empty-handed. And how would she explain the dress? Poppy would say she had stolen it out of a shop and had put it on after. Sure. They'd believe that, wouldn't they?

As Poppy approached the Willow, she could hear boisterous singing from various parts of the resort and yelping and barking from the pits where gamblers brought dogs to fight. She headed down the dark stairway to the cellar hole where she lived. She thought of Justin's goat and her little shed and how Justin tended her. *He'd never let anyone hurt that goat,* she thought. But Justin came from a different world.

The door to Ma's room burst open before Poppy had a chance to open it herself.

"Where have you been, lady?" Ma grabbed Poppy by the hair and pulled her into the room. "You've been gone all day, and you'd better hand over money to me. I'm not puttin' up with you if you don't come through." She was about to clout Poppy once she had her inside the room, but she stopped, her arm in midair. Ma's expression changed in the lantern light as she looked at Poppy's dress. "Well, lookey here! Girls!" she called to the others, who were standing by the beds. "See how fancy our little Poppy is in her new getup. Where did you get that new dress?"

"I was sick of wearin' the same old dirty dress and apron. So I stole this. It's mine and I got it for myself." She tossed the satchel onto the bed next to Renee. "Here, you can have my old clothes. I'm wearin' this from now on."

Ma's eyes narrowed. "I know what you did, you little sneak. You picked a few pockets—that's what you did. And then you went into a store and bought that dress— with money you should have brought home to me. That money was rightly mine! And you used it on yourself!"

The four girls gasped and huddled together.

For an instant Poppy wanted to say, *None of the money you get is rightly yours! It's all stolen!* Instead she said, "I didn't spend any money for this dress. I told you, I *stole* it!"

The palm of Ma Brennan's hand came across Poppy's cheek like a knife. "You ungrateful little liar! After all I've done for you—givin' you a home and food on the table."

She pushed Poppy onto the floor. "Take that dress off. You're givin' it to little Renee here. You put on your other clothes, missy. The ones you feel aren't clean enough or nice enough." She gave Poppy a kick. "Do it now!"

Poppy held back the tears she felt coming. She knew how Ma felt about tears—Poppy would get more slaps if she cried. So she took a deep breath and said, "This dress is the nicest thing I've ever had. Why should I give it away? It's mine!"

"And the money you used to buy it was *mine*!" Ma yelled. "Take it off before I hit you again."

Poppy tried to unbutton the back of the dress but couldn't reach.

"See? She had to have bought that outfit. She had someone help her into it!" In the lamplight, Ma's face was wrinkled with rage.

"I'll help you unbutton it," Julia said as she knelt on the floor next to Poppy.

Poppy let Julia undo the buttons and pull the garment over her head. The green ribbon that Claire had used to tie Poppy's hair back came tumbling off and fell to the floor.

"There!" Ma said. "The dress is yours, Renee. You're about the same size as Poppy, maybe a little smaller. Now, Poppy, you get into bed. I'll deal with you more tomorrow. Everyone else had supper. You'll go without. Maybe gettin' a little hungry will give you some appreciation for all I've done for you."

Dressed only in her underwear, Poppy climbed into the bed she now shared with Julia and Renee. Her face smarted and her knees bled where Ma had pushed her to the floor. But she held back the tears and the angry words she wanted to scream.

I'm getting out of here tonight, she thought, *as soon as everyone falls asleep.*

But where would she go? There was no one to take her in. No one she could trust or turn to.

I'll find a place. And I'll hide there until I know what to do. I'll never live here with Ma Brennan again. She remembered Ticktock's clean little shed and the bright quilt hanging on the wall. *That's where I'll go,* she decided.

CHAPTER TWELVE

- Claire's Warning -

"What happened to you?" Charlie asked Justin when he walked in the door.

Father jumped up. "Justin, did you get into a fight?"

"Your pants are torn and . . . you're bleeding!" Mother grabbed a clean dish towel, ran water over it, and began wiping the dirt from Justin's knees, which were poking through his ripped trousers.

"Two boys got hold of me," Justin told her. "Patrick Cahill and Four Fingers Foley."

"Not those ruffians!" Charlie shook his head. "Man alive! You sure got yourself into a fine fix."

"I'll bet you went right down to Wells Street, despite what I said," Mother muttered.

"I didn't want to let Poppy go down there by herself." Justin cringed as his mother swabbed iodine on his cuts.

"That girl can take care of herself," Father said. "She's one of them."

Claire, who had been standing by quietly, finally spoke up. "I think Justin was trying to protect her—like a gentleman should."

"He shouldn't be associating with anyone like her," Charlie said. "She's trouble."

"Well . . . just because she's poor doesn't mean she's trouble," Claire argued. "I think there's good in her."

"Oh, you'd think there was good in . . . the devil himself," Charlie said.

"I think there's some good in everyone," Claire shot back.

"That's 'cause you're marrying a preacher," Charlie insisted. "You're a dreamer, Claire."

Claire was about to flare up when Mother interrupted.

"It's better to be like Claire, Charles, and to look for the good in everyone."

Charlie is such a know-it-all, Justin thought as he sat at the table. Mother served him up a bowl of stew. "Let's not talk about Poppy anymore," he said. "I'd just as soon forget everyone from Conley's Patch."

No one spoke for a while, and then Justin changed the subject. "So, how did Mrs. Palmer like the emerald, Father?"

"She thought it was just the thing," Charlie answered.

"I was asking *Father*," Justin snapped. He'd had enough of Charlie for one night.

"Yes, she was pleased," Father agreed. "She likes the setting, so now I just have to secure the emerald into the pendant." He looked over at Charlie. "Mrs. Palmer wants me to create a tiara in diamonds for a Christmas party. Why don't you do a few designs, Charlie? It would be good practice, and I think you'd come up with something she'd like."

Charlie grinned, obviously happy with his father's suggestion. "Do you really think I have the artistic flair that you do?"

There he goes, hinting for more compliments, Justin thought.

Why doesn't Father give me a chance to design something? It's always Charlie!

"Absolutely," Father said. "When I retire, I want to be sure my son . . ." He cleared his throat. "I mean, *sons* . . . will carry on. In fact, I'm hoping our business will become well known throughout the country. Perhaps you'll open a shop in Boston, or New York—"

Justin interrupted. "Maybe I could be in charge of one of them?"

Charlie laughed. "And will you bring your goat with you? I can see it now. New York City. 'Butterworth's Jewelry' in big letters." He gestured grandly with his hands. "And a goat tied up by the doorway."

Everyone at the table burst out laughing—except for Justin. "I'm going out to check on Ticktock," he grumbled. "And if I ever had a business, yes, I would bring her. She's a lot better company than some people I know." He picked up a lantern from the side table and headed out.

"Don't get that goat excited," Father called after him. "Each time you go out there at night, she cries for an hour after you leave."

When Ticktock heard Justin coming, she ran to meet

him. He set the lamp on the fence post and undid the latch. As soon as the gate opened, the little goat pushed her head under Justin's arm.

"You are my best friend, aren't you, girl?" Justin whispered. "Did you hear them all laughing at me in there?" Justin put his cheek against Ticktock's neck and the goat nibbled on his collar. *Charlie makes me spitting mad,* Justin thought. *He's such a bigwig with his sales pitch and his smooth talk. Father says Charlie will run the store someday. He doesn't even consider that maybe I could be a jeweler. Nobody gives me a chance to do anything except sweep the floor. I'll bet Charlie doesn't know half as much as I do about geology and gemstones and their cleavage and refraction. . . .*

Justin rubbed his belly where Fingers had punched him. "And then there's Poppy. Father and Charlie think I'm plumb loco to be bothered with her," Justin said aloud. "Maybe I was stupid to go down to Conley's Patch, but I was trying to do the right thing and not leave Poppy when those tough eggs showed up." Justin sniggered when Ticktock's tongue tickled his ear—but only for a second, because tears came rushing into his eyes. He fought to hold them back. No way would he cry. Only sissies and babies cried. He'd be called a sissy for sure if Charlie saw him crying.

"I'll be okay, Ticktock," he murmured. "I'll show them all someday . . . I'll do something that will make them real proud—and sorry, too—for treating me like that."

"Justin?" Claire was standing by the fence. "Are you hungry? I brought you a pastry."

Had she heard what he'd been saying to Ticktock? "I've had enough pastries," Justin said, "but thank you."

"Are you all right, Justin?"

"I'm fine." Justin jumped up and brushed off his hands. "I was just saying good night to Ticktock."

"She's sweet and I can see why you love her." Claire opened the gate, came into the enclosure, and then sat on the threshold into the shed. "Come here, Ticktock." The little goat turned and headed to Claire to nuzzle her hand. "It looks like your goat wants the pastry."

"Let her have it. I'm not hungry," Justin said.

Claire held it out and the goat took it eagerly but gently from her hand. "Good girl. Good, sweet little kid," Claire crooned. Ticktock's tongue flickered out, looking for more.

"You did the right thing, staying with Poppy," Claire said.

"I know."

"Poppy shouldn't be living down there. Did you go to her house?"

"No. She insisted I leave. She said Ma Brennan would take care of her."

In the lamplight, Justin could see sadness in Claire's face. "Poppy cried and told me all about her life when she was in my room. She doesn't want to live with Ma Brennan. She wants to run away."

"Who's Ma Brennan, anyway?"

"Ma Brennan teaches girls to steal for her." Claire stood up. "From what I've heard, Ma Brennan is a wicked woman."

"Poppy told me Ma Brennan beats her." Justin swallowed the lump he felt in his throat. "I . . . I kind of feel sorry for her. She's tough but . . ."

"She's had to be tough to survive. If that woman is Poppy's guardian, the poor child hasn't had much of a life. No wonder she fell apart when I gave her a dress. She's never had any loving attention."

Justin felt a sick feeling in his stomach. "Do you think Poppy is a . . . pickpocket? Do you suppose she'd steal *from us*?"

Claire put her arm around Justin's shoulder. "I think Poppy is torn between *wanting* to do what's right and *having* to do what's wrong. I so wish I could help her." Claire bent over and kissed her brother's cheek. "You must be careful, Justin. You don't know where this friendship with Poppy might lead you—especially if she lives under Ma Brennan's thumb."

LATE MONDAY NIGHT,
OCTOBER 2, 1871

CHAPTER THIRTEEN

- *Poppy's Safe Place* -

Poppy waited until she was sure everyone was asleep. Then, moving quietly, she rolled off the mattress and onto the floor where her clothes had been thrown.

No! She would not wear those old, raggedy clothes again. Claire had given *her* the pretty dress and she wanted it back. Cautiously, she crept to the tattered armchair where Ma had tossed the new dress. Poppy reached for it silently and slipped it over her head. She couldn't reach the buttons, but it didn't matter. This was *her* dress and she'd never give it up. She felt through a pile of clothes on the floor until she found an old knit-ted sweater. She put her arms into the long sleeves and buttoned it in the front.

Carrying a shoe under each arm, Poppy crawled to the door and pulled it open an inch at a time. Once, Ma snorted, and Poppy froze, waiting to hear Ma's even breathing again. Then she opened the door gradually until her eyes became accustomed to the darkness and the stairway leading up to the street door became visible in the murky shadows.

Up one step, then another. One step, then another. The noises of wild laughter and revelry had ebbed, and Poppy knew it had to be close to dawn. She had to get far away before she was missed. If Ma woke up and found her leaving, Poppy would never escape and Ma would surely beat her until she was black and blue.

Poppy reached the front door and released it slowly. The night air swept in on a cool breeze, and the moon-light cast a soft glow on the street. Poppy closed the door quietly behind her, then sat on the front steps to put on her shoes. She tiptoed down to the dirt street and onto the board sidewalk, and then she scurried up the block toward Justin's house.

Two dark shadows stood on the corner of the block,

so Poppy squeezed into an alley. She shivered in the cold wind, waiting until the shadows disappeared into the night. *I hope no one stops me or grabs me,* she thought. She had heard stories about the vicious hoodlums who stalked the streets of Chicago day and night—hiding in places even worse than Ma Brennan's.

Breathlessly she darted to the main road, her shoes clickety-clacking and echoing on the dark streets.

At last, she saw Justin's house in the distance, on an acre of farmland. The house was dark, but it stood out silent and silver in the moonlight.

She tiptoed to the fence where Ticktock was kept, unlatched the gate, and opened it quietly.

Ticktock heard her and trotted out of her little shed, whimpering and bleating. Poppy looked toward Justin's house. There were no lights on and no one seemed to be stirring. The sound of Ticktock's whines hadn't carried that far, she hoped.

"Hush, Ticktock," Poppy whispered, bending down to pet the goat. "It's just me, Poppy." The stars glistened above the pasture, and the lawn and trees were swathed in moonlight. How still it was. Not a harsh sound—nothing but the wind.

As Poppy went into the shed, Ticktock trotted close behind her, bleating eagerly again as she butted Poppy's backside. Poppy giggled. "You silly little goat."

Inside, the hay smelled sweet. Poppy reached for the quilt, lay down on the bed of straw, and pulled the blanket over her. Ticktock nibbled at the fabric. "No, no, Ticktock," she whispered. "Come here."

The goat came closer and nudged her hand, as if requesting for Poppy to pat her. Poppy scratched the goat's head and neck and then pulled Ticktock down next to her.

"Let's go to sleep. I need to get up and leave before someone finds me." She fixed the quilt over both of them. "There." Ticktock seemed to understand, because she folded her legs and leaned against Poppy. Soon the little goat dropped her head and became quiet.

Poppy put her arms around Ticktock. "You're my first best friend, Ticktock," she whispered. "I wish I could stay here with you forever."

She closed her eyes, and for the first time ever, she felt safe—at least for a little while.

CHAPTER FOURTEEN

- Not Yet -

"Blaa! Blaa!" Justin pulled a pillow over his head and tried to go back to sleep, but Ticktock's insistent bleats came through. He pushed the pillow aside and glanced out the window by his bed. The very first streaks of dawn spread across the horizon in red and orange bands. *I wonder what's wrong with Ticktock. She usually doesn't start calling this early. She must still feel strange in her new home. I better get up before she wakes everyone.* He climbed out of bed barefoot and tiptoed down to the kitchen.

"What's going on with Ticktock?" Claire was

already up and lighting the kitchen stove. She had on a blue striped robe over her nightclothes. "Were you just out there? She's crying like she does when you leave her."

"No. I've been in bed." Justin went outside, where the dawn was now taking over the sky and birds had begun to chirp in the trees.

"Blaa! Blaa!" cried Ticktock. She was standing by the gate, crying.

"What's wrong, little nanny?" Justin asked soothingly. The little goat eagerly pushed her way through the gate the moment Justin opened it. "No, no," Justin said, closing the opening. "Are you hungry?" He went into the shed and opened the barrel that contained the goat's food. "Here you go." He was about to pour food into Ticktock's tin basin but stopped in surprise. The bowl was almost full. "What's this? I filled this last night and it was almost empty when I left."

Claire, still in her robe and slippers, came into the shed and had apparently overheard Justin's words. "Is Ticktock all right? Didn't she eat last night?"

"Yes, she did. She ate so much, I didn't want to leave any more in the basin. Look." He pointed to the food in the bowl. "It's just about full." He turned to his sister. "Did you feed her after I went to bed?"

"No, of course not. But perhaps Father or Charlie did when she started bellowing."

"I don't think so. I would have heard them. Besides, if she's not hungry, why is she bleating? Do you suppose she's sick?"

"No," Claire said. "Look at her. She's ready to play now that you're here. Maybe she was lonely."

Justin sat down on the doorsill and hugged his pet. "I wish you could talk and tell me what you want."

"Look, Justin." Claire pointed to the quilt, which was folded neatly on the hay. "Who do you suppose folded this blanket?"

Justin frowned. "I keep it on the shelf unless it's real cold. How did it get folded like that? Do you think someone was in here?"

"It had to be *somebody*. I don't suppose Ticktock climbed up, took it off the shelf, and then folded it," Claire said with a wry grin.

"Whoever it was is gone now."

"And that would explain why Ticktock was crying. Whoever was with her left, and she became lonely."

Claire bent down and examined the flattened bed of hay. "Someone other than Ticktock slept here. Do you suppose you walked in your sleep?"

"No!"

"Then who could it have been?" Claire was silent for a moment. Then she nodded. "Oh, Justin, I think it was—"

"Poppy." Justin spoke his sister's thoughts. "But why? She went home."

"Perhaps she was punished for being late," Claire said. "Heaven knows what might have happened when Poppy got home."

Justin scratched his head. "But to sleep in a goat's barn? Surely she must have somewhere else to go."

Claire shook her head. "If she had somewhere else, she'd have gone there."

"Do you suppose she'll come back tonight?"

"I think she will. But don't wait up and confront her, Justin. Let her come. Maybe we can put some food out here for her—as if we left it by mistake."

"Suppose Mother or Father or Charlie finds out? They know she's from Conley's Patch. They'd send her packing. We can't tell them."

"No, the poor thing needs to figure out what she's

going to do. Meanwhile, we won't say anything to any-one. She's careful about coming here late and leaving early." Claire sighed. "I wish I could help her find a good place to stay."

"She doesn't like goats," Justin said. "She thinks they stink. She'd better be good to Ticktock."

"She doesn't have a mean streak in her body. If she were mean, do you think Ticktock would have cried so much when she left? It looks to me like Poppy fed your goat." Claire sat next to Justin and put her arm around his shoulder. "I think Ticktock is fond of Poppy. And Poppy needs a friend. The goat is most likely the *only one* she can trust right now."

"Do you think . . ."

"Yes, I think eventually Poppy will come to us for help. But she's not ready yet."

CHAPTER FIFTEEN

- *Poppy's Worst Fear* -

It was still dark when Poppy left the goat house and headed toward town. Her stomach grumbled for something to eat. In fact, she was so hungry that she began to wonder if she'd done the right thing by leaving Ma Brennan's. After all, despite the beatings, at least she had something to eat every day. Where could she go now to stop this awful, empty ache in the pit of her belly? She had no money.

Of course! I'll get some money from the hiding place behind the rock and have a good breakfast at a real restaurant!

She brushed off bits of hay from her new dress and then straightened out the wrinkles as well as she could. *I wish I had a comb,* she thought as she drew her fingers through her hair.

Poppy headed up the street toward Conley's Patch, hoping no one would see her. The eastern sky was lighter now. A rat scurried across her path and she heard someone crying in one of the alleys as she passed by. That morning, when she had awakened in the goat barn, the sounds had been different—the warbling of birds, the sound of wind rustling through the dry meadow grass, Ticktock's soft bleating. Tonight, when it was really late, she'd go back there. That would be her secret, safe place. But she'd need to be careful so that no one would know she'd been there.

She paused, thinking about her rush to leave that morning. Had she folded the quilt and put it back on the shelf, the way she found it? Had anyone heard her pump water for herself and for Ticktock? When she poured food into Ticktock's tin basin, it had clattered loudly. She'd need to be more careful from now on.

She reached the empty lot and old foundation. Poppy found the loose stone, stretched her arm into the hole, and pulled out the can where she'd hidden the money.

She removed the matchbox carefully, so as not to crack the wax. Then she took one dollar and put the rest back into the can.

After replacing the stone, she returned to the street.

She remembered a small café where they served coffee and breakfast. As she headed up the walkway, she heard the familiar sound of clanging bells, hissing steam, and galloping hooves. She stopped as sweating horses pulling a fire engine clattered by. The engine stopped a little ways up the street, and Poppy could now see fingers of flames sputtering from an old wooden building, casting sparks everywhere. A hot cinder landed on her shoulder. *Slap!* She brushed it away, searching to see that it hadn't scorched her new dress.

She crossed to the other side of the street and paused to watch two firemen pumping a water tank on the truck, while another man shot water from a hose onto the burning building.

As black smoke that was swept by the wind blocked her vision, she ran between gusts until she could see the little café where she was headed.

Once inside, she took a seat far away from the window, for fear Ma Brennan or the girls might pass by and see her. When the waitress handed her a menu, she brushed it aside. She couldn't read anyway, so she asked, "How much for a glass of milk and a dropped egg on toast?"

"Fifteen cents. The milk is fresh—Mrs. O'Leary delivered it this morning."

"That's good," Poppy said with a little sniff, the way she'd heard some of the highfalutin ladies speak. "I can't abide sourin' milk."

Poppy waited, twiddling her thumbs. Some of the customers were reading the newspaper. Others talked about the weather.

"We have a problem with this drought," one man said, pointing to an article in the morning news. "This town is a tinderbox just waiting for a spark."

"Between the wooden buildings and the lumberyards, Chicago would be gone in a puff of smoke," agreed a young man at an adjoining table.

"Nothin' we can do 'bout it," his friend said. "Can't change the weather."

"They should have thought about fires when they put up all the wooden construction," the first man argued. "We got lumber mills and sawdust, wooden bridges, wooden houses . . ."

Even wooden sidewalks, thought Poppy.

A waitress came around to refresh their coffee. "The fire trucks are out near every day. Bob Williams, the fire marshal, told me that there were more than six hundred fires during the past two years."

The waitress set Poppy's order in front of her. The toast was cut in quarters, shiny with melting butter. The egg was perfect with the yolk just a little soft. Poppy pierced it with her fork and the yolk dribbled down into the bread. She grabbed a slice of toast eagerly and gobbled it down. After she finished the egg, she slathered the last piece of toast with strawberry preserves from a white covered dish. She ate it slowly this time, enjoying all the thick sweetness and sipping on the fresh, cold milk between bites. How wonderful to be able to buy food at a restaurant! Anything you want—all it takes is money. But the only way Poppy knew how to get money was to steal it.

She watched the men leaving the nearby table. One of them dropped a few pennies onto the tablecloth, as a tip for the waitress. Poppy reached over quickly and slipped the pennies into her own dress pocket. A few minutes later, the waitress came to clean the nearby table and went away with a look of disappointment on her face.

Poppy felt a bit sorry for the waitress but brushed the feeling aside. After all, Poppy had to live, too, especially now that she was away from Ma Brennan's. She needed to take care of herself.

Poppy wondered how much money she could make if she worked as a waitress. Waitresses made a small salary, she'd heard. But then they got tips—a few cents for themselves from good customers.

"Are you finished?" Poppy looked up as her waitress reached for the empty plate. "Is there anything else?"

"No," Poppy said. "Thank you."

The waitress put a tab of paper on the table. Poppy checked the bill. Two figures—a one and a five. That meant fifteen cents, just as she had been told. She took out her dollar to pay at the counter. She paused for a moment, then took the pennies from her pocket and placed them on the table. A tip for her waitress.

After paying her bill, Poppy stepped outside. The sun was shining brightly now. Most of the fire down the street was out, and the black clouds of smoke faded away in the breeze. She found a bench and sat down to be sure she had been given the correct change. It took her a while—she wasn't used to figuring out sums.

Suddenly she noticed two shadows appear on the ground in front of her. Looking up, she felt her heart drop. Four Fingers Foley and Patrick Cahill were standing before her.

"Where's your big-shot highfalutin bodyguard?" Fingers asked.

Poppy tucked the money into her pocket and then stood up to leave, but Patrick blocked her way. "Where did ya get the money, Poppy?" He tried to reach into her pocket, but she smacked his hand hard.

"Come on, Poppy," Fingers said. "We know what you're up to. You're makin' friends with that rich jeweler's kid. Now we're here to help you out."

Poppy frowned. "I don't need help."

"Sure you do." Fingers pushed her down onto the bench. "Let's talk. You're plannin' to cash in on your friendship with the Butterworths. They've got money and they own that jewelry store on State Street. Right?"

"Wrong!" Poppy stomped her foot. "I'm *not* friends with the Butterworths."

"Well, it looks to me like you're tryin' your best to be friends with that pantywaist Justin. Or is it the goat you like?" Patrick laughed. "He's crazy. He has a stinkin' goat for a pet."

"That goat does not stink!" Poppy snapped. "And Justin isn't crazy."

Fingers chuckled. "See, Patrick? She does like that Justin kid."

Once again Poppy tried to get up, and once again Fingers pushed her down. "Now, listen to me. We're all pals here and we're willin' to help you break into the jewelry store. And we're willin' to cut the sugar even."

"Who said I was goin' to rob the Butterworths?" This time Poppy jostled herself from Fingers and twisted from Patrick's grasping hands. She tried to bolt off, when she was stopped by a large, imposing figure. Ma Brennan!

"Aw, look who's here! It's my own little Poppy, who ran away from her ma last night." She held Poppy by the shoulders. "Are these boys giving you trouble, dearie?"

A sinking feeling of hopelessness swept over Poppy. She could never get away from Ma Brennan. Right now all she could do was act as if she were sorry—and find out what Ma intended to do.

"They're scarin' me, Ma," Poppy whimpered as Ma put her arms around her. "Make 'em go away."

"Those no-accounts were threatenin' you. I heard every word. Don't worry, Poppy. Ma's here now and she's goin' to protect you."

The boys backed away as Ma shook her fist at each of them. "Leave my Poppy alone or you'll disappear one of these nights," she warned. "Scram! Get outta here!"

Fingers and Patrick took off up the street, and Ma pulled Poppy down onto the bench. "Now, you tell me why you ran away from your ma, who's loved ya all these years. I scared you last night, but you've gotta learn, dearie, that you mustn't steal from your ma and buy things with *her* money. It's not nice." She put her arms around Poppy. "Let's let bygones be bygones."

Poppy knew Ma very well, and she knew Ma only *sounded* forgiving. But Poppy knew how to pretend, too. "I'm sorry I ran away, Ma. But you scared me. And I really, truly didn't steal your money to buy this dress. The Butterworths gave it to me."

"So it's true, then, that you're a friend of the Butterworth family? The ones that own the jewelry store?"

"I guess so. I went to see their son Justin's pet goat."

"You went to visit a goat?" Ma laughed her toothless smile.

"Yes, and then they invited me to supper and gave me this dress."

"Well, I have a job for you, Poppy. I want you to stay friends with that Butterworth boy and his folks. Yep. Then I want you to do one simple thing. I want you to get me a key to the Butterworths' jewelry store. That's all you have to do."

So that's what Ma is after—a key. I'll never tell her I already have a wax of the key. But how could she do this to the Butterworths, who had been so good to her? Why, she almost felt like a good person herself when she was with them.

"I don't want to do that, Ma," Poppy said. "I don't want to steal from them."

"Oh, my! Our little Poppy suddenly has that thing they talk about in church: a conscience. Now you've got God, too, I suppose."

"I ain't never gone to church, as you know. And I don't know God. But I know one thing. I like them people— the Butterworths. And I ain't goin' to steal from them."

"I didn't ask you to steal. All you have to do—*like I just said*—is get me a key or a copy in wax. No one will ever know it was you." Ma didn't seem sweet anymore.

Her eyes narrowed and she was beginning to sound like her usual mean self.

"I can't!" Poppy said, getting up from the bench. "And I won't!"

"Oh, tsk-tsk. That's too bad. I'd hate to think something bad would happen—maybe to that cute little goat." Ma grabbed Poppy by the arm, her fingers clutching so tightly that Poppy winced. "Here's the deal. You do what I say and that little goat will be happy and healthy. If you don't . . ." Ma's face darkened and her voice was icy cold. "I hear goats make a real nice juicy stew."

Poppy's stomach turned and she felt as if she might faint. "No! Don't you touch Ticktock. I'll do whatever you want, but don't you lay a finger on her!"

CHAPTER SIXTEEN

- *Mew* -

"Do you want scrambled eggs and a slice of ham, Justin?" Claire asked her brother once they were in the kitchen.

"Yes, I'm hungry."

"We were both up before dawn. Here, have some tea while I make breakfast." She poured tea from the large teapot that was always simmering on the stove.

"Remember," Justin reminded her, "don't say anything to anyone about someone sleeping in the goat house. Father or Charlie would stay up all night watching and would scare anyone away—and Mother would be frightened."

"I won't say anything yet," Claire promised. "But first we need to be sure it really was Poppy."

"What about Poppy?" Charlie appeared in the doorway. He yawned. "Pour some tea for me, too, Claire."

Justin hoped his brother hadn't heard him speak about the goat shed. He gave Claire a warning glance as she handed tea in a china cup to Charlie.

Charlie helped himself to cream and took a sip. "So?" he asked. "What about Poppy?"

"I was telling Justin how sorry I feel for the poor girl. She's never had a decent dress in her life, I swear," Claire answered.

"Hmm. Probably not." Charlie seemed to lose interest. "Justin, after school today, Father wants you to come down to the store. He thinks you need to learn more about the business, and there's some book work and tagging that needs to be done."

Justin raised his eyebrows. "You mean he wants me to do something besides sweeping and cleaning?"

"Yes, you've been promoted," Charlie replied. "You were so upset last night, storming out of here, that he felt unhappy for you."

"Oh, Charlie," Claire said as she poured the eggs into

the pan. "Father realizes that Justin is old enough to start taking on responsibilities at the store, same as you." She nodded to the ham leg that lay in another pan on the stove. "Slice up some of that ham for us, Charlie. You're not exempt from helping out around here, you know."

"Claire, the perfect parson's wife," Charlie said with a smirk. He found a sharp knife and cut ham slices. "So get down to the store after school, Justin."

"All right, I will." Justin was certain he didn't want Charlie as his boss. But at least Father had noticed that Justin wanted to be included in the family business, too.

I'll show Father and Charlie that I can handle just about anything in that store!

Father and Mother came into the kitchen just as someone knocked on the back door.

Justin could see the top of his friend Randy's slicked-down brown hair. "It's Randy from up the road," he said as he got up to open the door.

"What's he doing here so early?" Mother asked. "And you've all had your breakfast already. What's going on?"

Justin opened the door and laughed out loud. "Look what Randy's got for you, Claire!"

Curled up in Randy's arms was the tiny, fluffy black

kitten. Justin bent closer to look and could hear the kitten purring softly.

"Oh, my darling little kitty!" Claire whispered as she gathered the kitten into her arms. "Look at her beautiful amber eyes. Isn't she sweet?"

"There's nothing as lovable as a kitten," Mother agreed. "But she's so little. Is it all right to take her from her mother so soon?"

"She'll be fine," Randy said. "She does suck on my finger sometimes, but Mother says she'll get over that habit soon."

"What will you name her?" Father asked Claire.

The kitten began to mew and knead with her little claws. "I'll name her Mew," Claire said. "My little Mew." She held the kitten up and then kissed her nose. "I know what I'll do—I'll keep you inside my pocket, where you'll feel warm and loved." Claire put the kitten into her apron pocket. "She'll stay safe and warm and close to my heart. Thank you, Randy."

Mother chuckled. "She'll be loved, that's for certain."

"She'll grow to be the church cat that will take care of all the poor church mice," Father said, laughing.

The kitten mewed and wiggled until Claire stuck her

finger down into the pocket. The kitten became silent. "She's nursing on my finger!" Claire said softly.

"Well, are you ready for school, even though it's early?" Randy asked Justin.

"Let's go," Justin said, slipping into his pea jacket. "I'll see you at the store after school, Father."

"No, I'm staying home today. I'm letting Charlie take over the shop."

"Oh, I thought you'd be there, too." Justin couldn't help showing his disappointment.

"It'll be a test for him to see how he handles being the new manager." Father winked at Charlie, and Charlie gave everyone a broad grin. Obviously, Charlie had already known Father had given him the new title.

"Charlie's the new . . . manager?" Justin's throat tightened and he could hardly get the words out.

"Yes, he'll be your boss today." Father must have noticed Justin's face fall. "Don't worry, son," Father said quickly. "Charlie won't be a harsh taskmaster."

Justin shot an angry glance at his brother as he went outside with Randy, slamming the door behind him.

"*Nobody* is going to be my taskmaster," Justin muttered. "Especially Charlie."

CHAPTER SEVENTEEN

- *Poppy's Dilemma* -

Ma Brennan didn't waste a minute. "I'm givin' ya till Friday to get a key to the Butterworths' jewelry store. Before the time is up, I want that key *in my hand* . . . or else. You know what will happen."

Poppy nodded.

"Once we're inside the store, Mr. Plant's cracksmen will know what to do with the safe. They'll either break it or take it." Ma laughed. "That's good! How big is the safe?"

"I don't know anything about the safe. You said all

I need to do is get you a key. So don't ask me about the safe."

"No back talk, missy. Or you'll get another smack across the face."

Poppy sighed. "If you slap me again, the family will know who did it. They know you're the one who's . . . bringing me up."

"Well, ain't that too bad. Poor, poor little Poppy." Ma put her face close to Poppy's. "That's all the more reason for them to feel sorry for ya. You'll be so pathetic, they'll take ya right under their wing." Ma straightened Poppy's dress. "Looks like they already have. They gave ya this nice dress, didn't they? And ya spent the night there, too. Why, you're practically a member of the family!"

"I wish I were," Poppy mumbled.

"Go!" Ma shoved her. "Go up there and do what ya have to do . . . or that little goat—"

Poppy felt sick again, as if her stomach were about to upchuck her breakfast. "I said I'd do it!" she interrupted bitterly.

"There's my good girl. I'm the only family ya have. I've taken good care of ya ever since you were a babe." Ma gave Poppy a quick hug. "Now, off ya go to win over those Butterworths. Just be your sweet little self like I showed ya."

Poppy walked away and up the street toward Justin's house. Her legs didn't want to go that way. They wanted to run in another direction.

Why didn't I tell Ma I already had an impression of the key? Then it would be all over with. I'd never have to see Justin or Claire . . . or Ticktock again.

She thought of Ticktock, her wiggly tail, and how she'd cuddled next to Poppy the night before. *Oh, I'd just as soon die than have anything happen to Ticktock.*

Poppy thought about Claire and how she had held Poppy in her arms while Poppy had sobbed and cried. No one had ever held her like that.

Strange, come to think of it. She usually didn't think about anyone else's broken heart. But now Poppy understood how disappointed Claire would be if she knew Poppy had betrayed the family.

And if anything happened to Ticktock, Justin's heart would be broken, too—and so would Poppy's.

I know for certain that Ma wouldn't think twice about hurting that little goat. I'll have to do what Ma said. I'll have to give her the key.

Ma said no one would know I had anything to do with the robbery—that I wouldn't be stealing.

But I'd know. And I'll never feel right again if I help Ma steal from the Butterworths.

TUESDAY AFTERNOON,
OCTOBER 3, 1871

CHAPTER EIGHTEEN

- The New Man in Charge -

Justin had promised Charlie that he'd be ready to work at three o'clock. He reached Butterworth's Jewels and Timepieces just as the clocks inside began to chime.

Ding-Dong! The bells on the door sounded loudly as he entered, immediately followed by the tolling of the grandfather clocks. The hand-carved wooden German cuckoos and the banjo clocks all clamored at once.

"I'm here, Charlie! Right on time!"

"Just by the skin of your teeth!" Charlie, who had been polishing the glass, handed him a rag and a bottle of vinegar. "Here, finish wiping these countertops. They're covered with fingerprints." He nodded toward the office door near the back room. "When you're finished, come see me in the workroom."

Justin sighed and did as he was told. Then he followed his brother to the workroom, where his father repaired watches and jewelry.

He first had to walk through the office, where his father kept the safe and all the most valuable gems and timepieces. The large safe worked with a combination lock, and no one, except Father, knew the combination of letters that would open it. Justin often wondered if it was the name of one of the family members. Sometime, when no one was looking, he'd like to try it—just for fun.

"Come in here, Justin." Charlie had a large, velvet box and called him into the workroom. On the table by the window where his father repaired the jewelry were a list and a bag of tags. "You need to put price tags on all the new watch chains in this carton," Charlie said, depositing the jewelry box on the table.

"See this list?" Charlie continued. "There are two prices for each numbered item that you'll match up in the box. The first price is the wholesale price. Do *not* put that price on the tag. You must only put the *second* price—the *retail* price—on the tag."

Charlie demonstrated by taking a gold chain from the box. "Here's the number already on the tag. What does it say?" He showed it to Justin.

"B-one-one-eight-eight," Justin answered. This was an easy job. Why was his brother making so much over it?

"Now look on the list. See? Here's B-one-one-eight-eight. There are two prices, right?"

"Charlie, I'm not stupid. I can do this."

"Tell me which price you'll put on the tag for this chain, then."

Justin glanced at the paper and then spoke as if he were reciting from a first-grade book. "Dear me. The wholesale price is thirty-five dollars. The retail price is seventy dollars, and *this* is the price that I'll put on the tag."

"Don't be so flip. If you put the wholesale price on because you're not paying attention, Father will lose money. If it's wrong, whoever buys it will get a real bargain and Father will lose out."

"Very well, *boss*. I get it. I'll be careful. I'll pay attention. I'll put the retail price on the tags. Hmm, looks like a lot of jewelry here. Should take me the rest of the day. By the way, how much will I get paid for this very difficult work?" Justin asked in a wry tone.

Charlie rolled his eyes. "A fair wage, but only if you do it right. Pay attention. Retail versus wholesale." He went out into the shop, leaving Justin to do his work.

"I got it, I got it." *Charlie just loves being the manager,* he thought bitterly. Justin sat down and began to work. The sun shone through the window and gave him enough light to work quickly.

After about an hour, the late afternoon sun had dropped and the room became dusky. Justin lit a lantern and checked to see how many more tags he needed to mark. Two more pocket-watch chains and he'd be done. Hastily, Justin checked the list. One was fourteen-karat white gold and the other was sterling silver. He made out the tags and tied them onto the chains. Then he placed the jewelry in the large box and brought it out to the sales room.

"I'm done!" he exclaimed. "Where do you want these items?"

"They can go on display now. You know where they go."

Justin lit another lamp—it was dark in this part of the shop now. He put the items in display cases around the store, replacing empty spots where items had been sold.

"I'm heading home," he told his brother, finding him in the back room. "Are you coming?"

"I need to lock up."

At that moment the bells on the front door jingled. "I'll be in the sales room. Maybe I can sell something really expensive today and surprise Father," Charlie said in a low voice. "Wait for me, will you?"

Grudgingly, Justin went to the office to sit and wait.

"Good afternoon, Mrs. Ogden," Justin heard his brother greet the wife of a well-to-do Chicago banker.

"I'm looking for a gift, Charles. It's for my husband's anniversary as president of the Center Bank."

Mrs. Ogden talks so snooty—like she's got a hot potato in her mouth. Justin moved closer to the door so he could hear.

"That's quite an honor, ma'am," Charlie answered. "My father has a beautiful chronometer that just came in from New York City."

"Well, Frank already has a watch."

"And a very nice one, I'm sure," Charlie said. "I'm

only suggesting a chronometer because it is even more elegant . . . and of course, your husband is a prestigious man. Let me show it to you." Charlie went into his father's private office. Justin followed him as he opened the safe.

"How come you know the combination? Does Father trust you with it?" Justin asked with a frown.

"Well, I'm the manager now, so Father thought I'd need it." Charlie twisted the dial to various letters on the combination lock.

Justin could catch the first few letters: C-R-I. Whose name started like that? He watched more closely, but Charlie turned away so he couldn't see.

"What are you hanging over my shoulder for? If Father wanted you to know the combination, he'd have told you."

"I'm just waiting for you to open the safe so I can see the chronometer," Justin answered. "You know I love to see the good stuff in there."

Charlie turned the dial, opened the safe, and pulled out one of the drawers.

Justin watched as his brother opened a black box. Inside were several gold and silver pocket watches.

Charlie held one up for Justin to see. "Here it is! Look at the engraving on the cover. Father would be proud of me if I could sell this." Charlie headed toward the sales room. "Just watch the master at work."

Charlie's trusted with the combination to the safe. Charlie will end up running the store, and what will be left for me? I'll just end up sweeping all the time or posting those stupid tags that a first grader could handle. Justin decided to pay attention to his brother's sales pitch to Mrs. Ogden. Maybe he could learn something from listening to the conversation in the sales room.

"First of all, notice the many shades and colors of gold on the cover," Charlie was saying.

"It is a beauty," Mrs. Ogden agreed.

"I can guarantee that neither you nor anyone in Chicago has ever seen the likes of this. Let me explain the inside." Justin could hear a click as his brother opened the face. "This mechanism knows the number of days in each month and also accounts for leap years. When activated, the watch chimes the exact time using different tones to designate the hours, quarter hours, and minutes with a loud, clear pitch." Charlie demonstrated the gentle chimes.

Mrs. Ogden drew a deep breath. "Oh, it is lovely! What is this dial for?"

"That is the second hand. It actually shows the seconds passing, and it can be stopped for measuring times . . . in a race, for example."

"I see. And this dial with the moons?"

"The phases of the moon accurately move as the month passes—a most modern development you won't find in an ordinary pocket watch."

There was a long pause. Then Mrs. Ogden spoke. "And the price? I hope it's within my price range."

Justin smothered a laugh. *The Ogdens have so much money, they could buy out the entire state!*

"For you, a special price. Twelve hundred dollars, Mrs. Ogden."

"That's exorbitant!"

"Well, of course it's expensive," Charlie agreed. "This is a work of art with an unmatched mechanism."

There was a long silence.

Charlie finally spoke again. "If you think it's too much, take a look in the showcases. Perhaps you'll find something in your price range." Justin could hear his brother putting the chronometer back in its container.

"Besides, I believe I heard my father saying Mrs. Palmer is looking for a special gift. So it might be sold already. I probably shouldn't have shown it."

Justin put both hands over his mouth to keep from laughing. Mrs. Palmer was the richest and most powerful woman in Chicago. *Mrs. Ogden will* never *let Mrs. Palmer get that pocket watch,* he thought. He couldn't help admiring Charlie's salesmanship.

There was another long silence. Then Mrs. Ogden sighed. "Very well. I'll give you a check for it right now. But I want it engraved with these initials." Justin could hear the scratching of a pen and a rustling of paper. "There better not be a charge for engraving!"

"There'll be no charge for *you,* Mrs. Ogden."

"I would hope not."

When Justin heard the bells on the front door jingle as Mrs. Ogden left, he ran into the sales room. "Wow! Charlie! Wait until Father hears you sold that chronometer!"

"I think he'll be pleased. While I make out the sales slip and directions, why don't you sweep the front entry before we head home."

Another big day for Charlie, Justin thought enviously.

Father will be making him vice president of the company before long. He moved into the entry and was about to begin sweeping when he saw the small figure of a girl.

"Hi, Justin," she said.

It was Poppy.

CHAPTER NINETEEN

- Sheep and Shepherds -

Poppy took a deep breath and walked boldly up to Justin. "I was just walking by. How's Ticktock?"

"She's fine. Why?"

"Just wondering." Poppy stood near the front display window, shifting from foot to foot, not knowing what else to say. Ma Brennan had demanded that Poppy act like the poor little girl that everyone took pity on. But she couldn't fool Justin. Justin knew she was a tough street girl from Conley's Patch. He wouldn't be taken in by any act she might put on.

She put her hands on her hips, cocked her head, and said to Justin, "So you're still sweepin' the sidewalks. Don't you do anything else for your pa?"

"I just finished an important job in the back."

"Doin' what?"

"Tagging valuable jewelry with the retail prices."

"Valuable jewelry? Your father really trusts you with valuable jewelry?"

"Why wouldn't he?"

Their conversation was interrupted as Claire approached the entry. "Hello, Justin and Poppy." She carried a bag in one hand and held her other hand in the deep pocket of her coat. "I thought I'd come downtown and pick up some fixings for our chicken dinner tonight."

Poppy smiled timidly at Claire. Did either of them know she had spent the night in the goat house? She brushed her hands down her dress, trying to smooth down the wrinkles.

Claire didn't seem to notice. Instead, she opened the top of her coat pocket. "Can you guess what I have in here?" she asked Poppy.

Poppy stepped closer to examine what was inside. "Mew! Mew!" Poppy jumped back, startled. "Mew!"

came another squeak, and then a dozen wiggles as the kitten climbed up to the opening.

"Oh! It's a tiny cat!" Poppy exclaimed as the little whiskered face peeked out at her.

Claire and Justin both laughed. "Her name is Mew. Here, you can hold her." Claire gently lifted the kitten from her pocket and placed her in Poppy's outstretched hands.

Poppy couldn't speak. This was the adorable, soft, and lovable kitten she'd always wanted. The kitten purred loudly in her arms and then took a section of Poppy's dress in her mouth and began to suck on it.

"She thinks you're her mother," Claire said softly.

"She's so . . . beautiful," Poppy finally said, finding her voice, which cracked with emotion. "I wish . . ." She was about to say, "I wish she were mine," but of course, this was Claire's kitten.

"I'm on my way home to make dinner. Forrest is coming tonight." Claire turned to Poppy. "Forrest Belmont is the minister at the Methodist church on Wabash Avenue. We're getting married soon."

Poppy nodded without answering. She had heard Claire would be married, but she hadn't known to whom. She didn't know what a minister did and she knew nothing about the Methodist church, other than she passed it when she was on Wabash Avenue. In fact, she'd never been in a church. But she'd heard that people sang songs and talked about God there. Poppy was told there were real gold crosses and valuable things in churches.

Ma always spoke nastily about the one time she had taken her girls to a church. Ma said there'd been a plate that was passed around to collect money from everyone. When Ma and the girls grabbed handfuls of money from the plate, they were ushered out of the church and told never to come back. Ma hated churches ever since.

That was all Poppy knew about churches. Claire's husband-to-be was a minister. "What's a minister?" she asked Claire.

"He's a servant of God who helps people—the shepherd who takes care of God's flock," Claire explained.

"A shepherd? Really? Do they keep sheep in the church?" Poppy asked.

Justin burst out laughing. Claire looked startled, but then she put her arm around Poppy. "Not real sheep, dear. They're people who are sheeplike. They follow their shepherd and his commandments obediently."

Poppy was confused. "Who's the shepherd?"

"God is the shepherd."

"I thought you said the shepherd was your minister friend Forrest?"

Justin laughed again. "He *thinks* he's God."

"That's not nice, Justin. Forrest is a dedicated servant of God," Claire snapped. Then, in a softer voice, she explained, "Forrest is a servant of the Good Shepherd, God. He acts as an earthly shepherd for God."

Poppy was even more confused. "What's in it for the sheep? What do they get out of it by following the shepherd?"

"Happiness, peace of mind, self-respect." Claire answered. "And a clean conscience."

There was the word that Ma Brennan had used: conscience. All this was too hard for Poppy to comprehend right now. The only word she understood a little was "happiness."

Meanwhile, little Mew was sound asleep in Poppy's arms. "We don't want to wake up the kitty," Claire said. "So I think you should carry Mew home for me. And then, maybe you'd like to help me make dinner. Would you like that?"

"Oh, yes!" Poppy replied quickly. To be with Claire and Ticktock and the kitten was the closest to *happiness* that she'd ever imagined.

TUESDAY EVENING,
OCTOBER 3, 1871

CHAPTER TWENTY

- Silver Versus Gold -

"I'll go home with Charlie," Justin said to Claire and Poppy as they headed down the sidewalk. He went back inside and to the workroom, where Charlie was examining a pearl.

"Mrs. Palmer is interested in pearls for her trip to Europe," Charlie said thoughtfully. "She wants a whole set—pendant, rings . . . I'd love to design the pendant. I wonder if Father would let me try." He looked up. "I heard Claire's voice. Is she here?"

"No, she and Poppy went home."

"She's with Poppy? Why does that child hang around here so much?"

Justin shrugged his shoulders. "I don't know. She likes Ticktock, I guess." He wouldn't tell Charlie that he and his sister suspected that Poppy had spent the night in the goat barn.

"Hmm. I think she likes *you*, not the goat," Charlie said with a wise-guy grin.

"Cut it out, Charlie. Are you going home soon?"

"As soon as you finish putting those chains into the display cases. I hope the prices on the tags are correct." They walked back to the sales room.

"Of course they are. And I'm already done."

The doorbell jingled as a young man entered. "May I help you?" Charlie asked.

"Yes, I'm looking for a chain for my pocket watch."

Charlie nodded and stroked his mustache. "Gold or silver?"

"Well, the watch is white gold." The man pulled the watch from a small pocket on his trousers. "Here." He laid the timepiece on the counter.

Charlie looked it over. "Hmm. Nice piece, but I don't believe this is gold. I think it's oxidized silver. I hope you didn't pay a lot for this."

The young man looked embarrassed. "It was a gift. I thought it was gold."

"I have silver chains here that are more reasonable than gold." He pointed to a few silver chains in the display cases. "Justin, pick out some silver chains and place them on the counter for this gentleman to see."

Justin sighed and unlocked the backs of the cases, looking at the silver chains he had just put away. It was easy to separate the white-gold chains from the yellow-gold chains, but the silver and white gold looked alike to him. *Oh . . . of course,* he thought, *the tags! The tags have the prices I marked, and white gold is more expensive than silver.*

Since most of the chains were alike, Justin picked out two that were different.

"These are silver," he said, checking the tags. "They're both eight dollars."

The young man examined each carefully, then picked up the chain that interested him the most. "This is the one I like," he said. "The smaller links look more expensive, and there are engravings of flowers on the clips at each end." He looked at the price tag. "Eight dollars is a fair price." He reached into a pocket and pulled out some bills. "I'll take this one and clip it to my watch right now."

Charlie took the money and put it in the cash drawer, but then he asked hesitantly, "May I see that chain first?"

The customer handed the chain to Charlie, who turned it over and over in his hand. He stared at the tag that Justin had made and looked puzzled. "One minute, please," Charlie said, and went into the back workroom, where Justin had tagged the items.

A gnawing worry cramped Justin's stomach. Had he put the wrong price on that chain? He didn't wonder for long, as Charlie returned to the sales room with the list of prices in his hand, his brow furrowed.

"I'm sorry," Charlie said with an icy glare at Justin. "The price on this chain was marked incorrectly. This is fourteen-karat white gold, not silver, and the correct price is eighty dollars, not eight dollars." He showed the list and item number to the customer, who looked it over gravely.

Justin felt as if he might throw up. He *had* marked the tag incorrectly! He'd never hear the end of it now, and . . . what would Father say when he found out?

The customer drew himself up tall. "You quoted me the price of eight dollars," he stated. "And the tag distinctly says eight dollars. I paid you eight dollars." He picked up the chain from the showcase counter and headed for the door. "So I will take my chain and leave." The bells on the door jingled as he left.

"Wait, wait!" Charlie called, running out after him. "You can't have that chain. Surely you know this is . . . highway robbery!"

Justin ran out right behind Charlie, but the man had already turned down another road and was out of sight.

"Well, you'll have to answer to Father about this," Charlie said. "Father checks profit and loss every week, and this will show a big red mark against Father's proceeds."

"Did you get the man's name?" Justin asked hopefully. "Is he a regular customer? Maybe Father knows who he is and can talk with him . . . maybe make a deal."

Charlie put his hands on his hips. "Well, aren't you full of good ideas!" he said mockingly.

"This was partly your fault, Charlie," Justin replied angrily. "You knew the watch was not gold. How come you didn't know the difference with the chains?"

"I counted on you to tag the chains correctly," Charlie answered back.

They went back into the store, and Charlie retrieved all

the watch chains Justin has displayed in the showcases. He dumped all the chains back into the original box. "Now I have to go over everything you've done to see if there are any more mistakes." He locked up the store, snuffed out the lanterns, and opened the front door. "Let's go home."

Neither boy spoke as they began to trudge the two-mile trek toward their house.

How I dread telling Father about the stupid mistake I made! Here I was, jealous of Charlie and trying to prove I can do everything just as well as he. Justin stopped in his tracks. "Charlie. Do we have to tell Father right away?"

Charlie seemed to think about this for a minute. "He'll find out. I told you, he checks profits and inventory every week, Justin."

"I'm sorry I flubbed everything up. I'm sorry I acted like such a know-it-all. I'll make it up to you and Father. I promise. Just don't tell him yet, Charlie. Give me a chance to make up for it. Please? After all, it's easy to mistake eight dollars for eighty dollars."

"It'll take years to make up for this mistake, Justin," Charlie muttered.

"I don't care if it takes forever. I'm feeling bad, Charlie, so don't be mean. "

Charlie kept on walking. Then he paused and turned around. "Here's what we'll do. You come with me tomorrow and we'll double-check the list. Maybe we can figure out a way to pay for that chain. But I can't keep this a secret from Father forever. He'll find out, Justin. And you better not blame me for any of this."

"None of it is your fault. It's all my fault," Justin admitted. "Maybe I can find the man who bought the chain and get him to pay us for it."

"Fat chance for that. We'll never see him again." Charlie started walking again. "Just how do you plan to pay Father back?"

"I don't know. I need some time to figure it out."

"Okay, but just for a few days. I won't put this sale on the books for now. But Father knows every single piece of inventory in this shop. When he finds out the chain is gone, he'll want to know the truth—that you made one huge mistake when you put the wrong price on that chain."

CHAPTER TWENTY-ONE

- *Supper at the Butterworths'* -

Mew was wiggling and crying in Poppy's arms, so she handed the kitten back to Claire. "I think she wants to go back into your pocket," Poppy said.

"She's warm and cozy and soon she'll fall asleep," Claire answered as she gently set the kitten back into her pocket. "I've been carrying her in here ever since Randy brought her over to our house. She feels safe when she's close to me."

Sure enough, by the time Poppy and Claire had walked one block, little Mew stopped crying. "Peek in here," Claire whispered, opening up the pocket slightly. Poppy peeped into the pouch. The kitten was curled up inside with her fluffy white-tipped tail wrapped around her face.

"I swear, she's the sweetest thing I ever saw," Poppy whispered.

"She's my baby—at least for now," Claire replied.

"Whatcha mean 'for now'?" Poppy asked with a frown.

"I meant she's my *baby* for now. Before you know it, she'll be all grown up."

"Will you love her when she's all grown up?"

Claire stopped walking and looked at Poppy curiously. "I'll love her always. I won't stop loving her, Poppy."

Poppy had to think about this. This lady would love her cat forever. But Poppy's mother loved *her* only for a little while, and then she gave her away to Ma Brennan. Ma Brennan never hugged Poppy or held her close and safe, the way Miss Claire cared for the kitten.

The wind gusted, howling between the buildings and driving dust and dirt through the air. Poppy could smell the familiar stink of the stockyards when the wind came up from the river.

Poppy had several bouts of coughing. "Are you all right, Poppy? Do you cough like this often?" Claire asked.

"I do when I sleep in my bed at home. The mattress we sleep on is on a dirt floor and . . ."

"Oh, goodness, that's unhealthy," Claire said with a gasp. "No wonder you have a cough. Does your mother give you medicine?"

"No, she don't give me medicine. She gets mad and slaps me real hard on the back. I get a-scared and it makes me cough more. So I put the pillow over my head so she can't hear me."

Claire stopped and put her arm around Poppy's shoulder. Poppy shivered and put her head on Claire's arm. "I wish she'd take better care of you, Poppy," Claire said. "I worry about you. Living in Conley's Patch is no place for a little girl. It's no place for anyone. There are so many wicked thieves and robbers who live there."

I live in Conley's Patch, Poppy thought. *I'm one of those wicked people.*

"Poppy, do you have any other relatives that might take you in and give you a good home? Did the city of Chicago give that Brennan woman guardianship of you?"

"I don't know," Poppy answered. "I was real little when my mother left me."

When they reached the Butterworths' house, the

sparkling stars were out and there were lights shining through the windows. *How nice it would be to always come home to a clean, pretty house like this one,* Poppy thought. "Can we check on Ticktock first?" she asked, and Claire nodded.

As they headed toward the goat's house, Claire pointed to a bright reddish star overhead. "That's Aldebaran. It's in the constellation of Taurus, the bull."

"There's a bull up there?" Poppy was puzzled. There were sheep in the church and a bull in the sky? Sometimes she couldn't understand what people were talking about.

Claire laughed. "Yes, there's a bull and a dog, a serpent, and a bear—all sorts of things up there in the sky. After supper I'll show you." Suddenly she grabbed Poppy's shoulder and pointed to the sky. "Look! A shooting star!"

Poppy looked up in time to see a brilliant trail of star-dust soar overhead. "It's real pretty," she said breathlessly. "I've never seen a shooting star in all my borned days."

"Make a wish," Claire said. "When you see a shooting star, you must make a wish."

Poppy thought of Ma Brennan and the girls and the others who lived at Under the Willow. How mean they could be if it suited them! She closed her eyes tightly and wished hard.

I wish Ticktock would be safe from Ma Brennan and her gang. Poppy didn't know if two wishes were permissible, but she made a second wish anyway. *I wish no one in this family would ever be hurt by them—or by me.*

As they approached the gated pasture, Ticktock bleated and ran to them. A bell jingled on her collar.

"Father bought Ticktock a collar with a bell," Claire said. "Now we know where she is all the time."

Even Mr. Butterworth cares about Ticktock, Poppy realized. *Everyone cares about everyone in this family.*

She and Claire leaned over the fence and Ticktock nibbled gently at their fingers. "Hello, you sweet nanny," Claire said, scratching the goat's head. She turned away, went up the back porch steps, and opened the kitchen door. When Poppy hesitated, she called, "Come into the house, Poppy. We'll visit with Ticktock after dinner."

Inside, Mrs. Butterworth was basting three large chickens she had pulled from the oven. The smell of chicken and herbs and stuffing filled the room. Mrs. Butterworth looked startled when she saw Poppy. "Oh, you've brought Poppy with you."

"She came by the store," Claire explained. "I thought she could use a nice chicken dinner."

Mrs. Butterworth smiled slightly. "Forrest is in the parlor with your father. Let me have your groceries," she said, taking the bag from Claire. "Oh, good. You bought butternut squash. And Poppy, would you like to mash the potatoes for me?"

"Yes, ma'am." Poppy nodded. "I'll be glad to help."

Claire placed little Mew in a basket near the warm stove. The kitten stretched and curled up to sleep again. Then Claire hung up her coat and put on an apron that was folded on the chair. She took Poppy to the sink and handed her soap. "Wash your hands first, Poppy."

After Poppy had washed up, Mrs. Butterworth set the pan on a rubber mat at the kitchen table along with a dish of butter. Poppy mashed the potatoes with a steel masher that Mrs. Butterworth gave her. "Put lots of butter in, too, Poppy. You don't need to skimp," she said.

After a few minutes, Mrs. Butterworth peeked into the pan. "Very good! You've made it as smooth as can be. Not a single lump!"

"At home I'd get smacked if I left a lump."

Claire, who had been busy cutting up butternut squash, took in her breath, and Poppy saw her give her mother a meaningful look.

When Poppy was finished, Claire said, "Come meet my fiancé, Forrest. He's in the parlor with my father."

But Poppy pulled back. Something felt very wrong. She didn't belong within this warm family circle—especially since Ma Brennan insisted she steal a key to the shop.

However, at that moment a tall man with a mustache entered the kitchen from the hall. "Darling, you're back!" He gave Claire a kiss on the cheek. "And who is this?" He smiled at Poppy.

"This is Poppy Brennan. She's a friend of Justin and Ticktock—and our little Mew. I invited her to stay for dinner." Claire turned to Poppy. "This is my fiancé, Pastor Belmont."

"I'm happy to meet you, Poppy." The pastor put out his hand and Poppy felt her face flush. No one had ever presented her so politely before.

She took the pastor's hand timidly. "How'dya do, sir." She spoke so softly, she hardly heard her own voice.

"Poppy's already mashed the potatoes, and now she'll help me set the table for dinner," Claire said. "Justin and Charlie should be along soon."

Claire and Mrs. Butterworth showed Poppy how to set the large dining room table with silverware. Claire didn't embarrass Poppy, who knew nothing of where the forks and knives should go and all that, although it did seem to Poppy that Mrs. Butterworth gave Claire long looks when Poppy didn't know where to put things.

There were china plates that all matched, and tall crystal goblets that Claire filled with a pitcher of water from the icebox. Mrs. Butterworth handed Poppy new white candles to put in real silver candlesticks. And when Mrs. Butterworth lit the wicks, the shining silver and glass sparkled in the candlelight.

The biggest surprise was the place set aside for Poppy—not at the kitchen table, but right in the dining room with the whole family.

Justin and Charlie arrived just as Claire carried a huge platter of chicken to the table, along with dishes of mashed potatoes and winter squash.

"Oh, I see Poppy's here," Father said when he came into the dining room. But Poppy could see a question in his eyes as he looked at his wife and daughter. *Well, no wonder,* Poppy thought miserably. *I am from Conley's Patch, and no one should ever trust me. Why, they probably think I'll walk off with a silver spoon or something.*

When everyone was about to sit at the table, she tugged on Claire's arm. "I think I should go now."

"No, dear," Claire said as she removed her apron. "Not until you've had a good supper."

After everyone was seated, Mr. Butterworth asked Forrest to say grace. Poppy had no idea what the word "grace" meant, but she watched everyone and did as they did, bowing her head as Pastor Belmont gave thanks.

Plates were passed, and Claire piled Poppy's high with food. Poppy watched until everyone else began to eat. Then she dug into the chicken and mashed potatoes, bolting down more food than she had ever eaten at one sitting. Claire patted Poppy's shoulder and smiled at her fiancé across the table, who grinned at her.

"It does my heart good to watch you eat, Poppy," Pastor Belmont said.

Poppy's mouth was too full to respond, so she swallowed water and sputtered, "I ain't never had such a good meal, mister." She wiped her mouth with her wrist, hating to dirty the neat linen napkin by her plate.

During dinner, Mr. Butterworth asked Charlie, "How did things go at the shop today?"

"I had a great day, Father. You know that chronometer

that we thought you'd never sell because of the price? Well, I sold it today to Mrs. Ogden."

"The full twelve hundred dollars?"

Charlie grinned. "All she wants is engraving on the back."

"Oh, my boy, you're a born salesman." Father smiled and winked at his wife. He turned again to Charlie. "Any other happenings at work?"

"Um, I was wondering if I might make a design for a pearl pendant. I understand Mrs. Palmer wants to take pearls on her trip to Europe."

"Well, yes—why don't you do a design on paper? Remember that you'll want to keep it simple, and not only because it will be for a pearl, which generally uses a simple setting. But I'm thinking it might be time for you to work with the gold itself."

"Oh, Father, that would be a great honor for me . . . I mean, to have one of my pieces in Mrs. Palmer's collection . . ." Charlie seemed suddenly at a loss for words.

"Don't put the horse before the cart, son," Mr. Butterworth said. "You haven't even designed it yet—"

"And Mrs. Palmer hasn't seen the pearl, let alone purchased it!" Justin interrupted.

"How about you, Justin? How did you do at the shop?"

"I, er . . . uh . . . I tagged the watch chains today—marked the prices and all that."

"I hope you did them right," Father said.

Charlie and Justin exchanged glances. "I was real careful, Father," Justin assured him. But Poppy noticed Justin looking down at his plate and making circles in his mashed potatoes with his fork.

Mr. Butterworth glanced at Poppy. "Were you in the store today, Poppy? Is that where Claire . . . picked you up?"

"Oh, no, mister," Poppy answered quickly, recalling how Mr. Butterworth and Charlie made her leave the day before, when she had gone to see Justin and Ticktock. "I was just walkin' by and saw Justin outside, so I stopped. And then Miss Claire came along."

Claire nodded. "That's when I invited Poppy to help me get supper. She set the table and mashed the potatoes. She did very well, didn't she?"

Mr. Butterworth didn't answer, but he looked at Claire for a long moment, and Poppy knew he wasn't happy that she was at their house for dinner. When Miss Claire invited her, Poppy should have said no. After all, she was just a guttersnipe from Conley's Patch. She reached for her goblet of water to take away the dry feeling in her throat, but her hands shook and drops of water spilled onto the white tablecloth. She took a deep breath and then stood up suddenly, nearly knocking over her chair. "'Scuse me. I'm gonna leave. I need to go home. Um, thanks for the dinner."

She ran through the kitchen and out into the dark night.

CHAPTER TWENTY-TWO

- *Time Will Tell* -

For a moment no one spoke after Poppy left. Justin's gaze went from Poppy's empty chair to his father, who was peering over the rim of his teacup at Mother. She glared at him accusingly. Charlie raised his eyebrows at Justin as if to ask, *What now?*

Pastor Belmont's eyes were on Claire, who seemed to be in shock. Then Claire broke the silence in a trembling voice. "We cannot let that child go back to that Ma Brennan and that awful place where she's been so badly treated all her life . . ." She jumped up and ran after Poppy.

Justin heard the front door open. "Poppy, wait! Please don't leave," Claire was calling. The door closed with a bang.

Again no one spoke. Then Father set down his teacup. "I'm sorry, but I just can't trust that child. She's from the Patch, for goodness sake, and she's hanging around Justin and the store—and now our house!"

"You made it very clear that she's not wanted here," Mother stated.

"I did not," Father replied. "I said nothing cruel."

"Your silence was loud enough," Mother said.

"You told me yourself you didn't trust her," Father went on.

"Maybe so, but I would never hurt her in any way . . . like you did," Mother said.

"How did I hurt her? I never said a word."

"If looks could kill, you killed her," Mother snapped.

"Poppy's not a bad person," Justin piped up. "I like her, even though she's kind of tough. It's like she doesn't know much about . . . things."

"Oh, she knows a lot about *things*," Charlie said. "She's been on the streets all her life."

"I mean, she doesn't know much about families and

friends and . . . those kinds of things." Justin found it hard to explain what he liked about Poppy.

Forrest spoke up. "Claire and I feel that with kindness and love, anyone can change and have a good life—if she chooses to."

"She's had enough kindness from *this* family," Father said.

"I can't help feeling sorry for Poppy," Mother said wistfully. "Besides, Claire is very fond of her."

"Claire's fond of everyone," Father argued. "She loves Poppy the way she loves the kitten. Poppy's cute, that's for sure. But she's a little wild thing, and like any wild thing, she'll eventually bite the hand that feeds her."

"Oh, for goodness sake, she's just a child," Mother argued.

"Yes, a child from Conley's Patch," Father responded. "Besides, she's older than she looks."

"Her life has made her older," Forrest said. "Self-preservation is the first law of nature."

"Time will tell who Poppy really is," Father said. "Now, what's for dessert?"

CHAPTER TWENTY-THREE

- *Special Words to Ticktock* -

Poppy was already out of the house, down the steps, and running to the main road when she heard Claire calling after her.

"Poppy, please wait for me. I need to talk to you. Don't run away like this. Come back."

Poppy stopped in her tracks. *Claire wants me to wait.* She felt a sense of relief. If she never saw Claire again, her heart would be broken in two. This was the very first time she'd ever had anyone she really cared about—or who cared about her. *Claire does care, doesn't she? At least she seems to. Or is she just being kind to a little guttersnipe?*

Poppy *had* to know for sure, so she waited for Claire to catch up with her.

"Poppy, dear, don't be sad or angry at my father," Claire said breathlessly as she approached Poppy. "He just doesn't understand people who come from . . . another . . . culture."

"You mean people like me—from Conley's Patch."

Claire nodded. "He's been robbed in the past, and that place out there where you live, that's owned by Roger Plant—it's a den of thieves and . . . worse."

"Is Mr. Butterworth afraid I will rob him, too?" Poppy asked.

"Probably. But I know you would never rob or betray anyone—especially those who care about you." Claire put her arms around Poppy and held her close.

Poppy hugged Claire tightly, afraid Claire might disappear if she let go. *What if Claire knew that Ma Brennan is planning to rob the jewelry store? What if she knew I have to give Ma a key to save Ticktock? Surely Claire would hate me if she knew.*

"Do you . . . really . . . care about *me*?" Poppy asked her.

"Of course I do. I thought you knew that without asking," Claire whispered. "But maybe you need to hear it—in real words." Claire pulled away and lifted Poppy's chin so they looked in each other's eyes. "Poppy, I care about you very much—in fact, I'm learning to love you." Claire's eyes filled with tears as she went on. "I want you to be happy and away from those people who have hurt you. I want to show you how good and happy families really live. I want you to know that you don't have to steal."

"But I have nowhere to live and no family. I've had to steal so's I can eat." She held back her own tears, but her mouth quivered. "I'm not part of your family, either, 'cause no one but you wants me around."

"Oh, you must know how much Justin likes you, Poppy. He teases you a little, the way boys tease their sisters. I've told Forrest all about you, and he wants to help you."

"But what shall I do? I can't go back to your house— not after what happened in there with all the 'spicious and hateful looks I got. "

And I can never go back to Ma Brennan's, she wanted to say. As if reading Poppy's thoughts, Claire spoke. "You mustn't go back to Conley's Patch. I'm going to suggest something, but I need to talk to Forrest about it first. In the meantime, perhaps for now . . . you might stay overnight with Ticktock—and that way you won't need to see my father again tonight."

Poppy almost blurted out that she had already spent one night in the goat barn but decided it didn't matter now. "I'd like to stay with Ticktock," she said, "but I don't want your father to find out."

"I won't tell him and he won't be going out to the goat barn. Ticktock is Justin's responsibility. Father's not a mean man, Poppy. However, he knows that Conley's Patch is full of thieves. After all, Father owns the biggest jewelry store in town, so he has to be cautious."

Poppy nodded. She understood only too well that Mr. Butterworth should be fearful and cautious. Plans were already being made to rob his jewelry store. No one from Conley's Patch could be trusted. *Not even me,* Poppy thought sadly.

"Come on, Poppy. I wish you could come sleep in my room, but for now, if you don't mind sleeping in the goat barn . . ."

"I don't mind, ma'am. I'll be quiet and . . . I'll cuddle

with Ticktock like I—" *Whoops!* She almost said, *Like I did last night,* but caught herself in time.

Claire took her hand and they walked back to the paddock. "Look at the stars, Poppy," Claire said. "I swear I just saw another shooting star. I wonder if there's a shower of stars tonight."

Poppy looked up in time to see another. "I saw one!" she exclaimed. "May I make another wish?"

"Of course. But don't tell what your wish is. It's a secret you share only with the stars."

Poppy closed her eyes and wished once again. *I wish that Mr. Butterworth's store will never be robbed,* she pleaded silently, and *I wish Ticktock will be safe from all harm.*

Claire opened the gate to the enclosure. The little goat bounded up to them, her bell jingling merrily. "You love Poppy, don't you, Ticktock?" Claire cuddled the goat. "You be a good girl and share your house tonight with her." Claire got up and whispered, "Poppy, tell Ticktock you love her."

Poppy was startled. Those were words too difficult for Poppy to say to anyone. "I . . . I don't know . . ."

"It's all right—I'll tell her," Claire said, bending over the goat and petting her head and nubby horns. "You are a sweet and gentle little nanny. I love you, Ticktock, and I know Poppy loves you, too." Ticktock butted Claire gently and then turned to push against Poppy.

Poppy, taken by surprise, lost her balance and fell. She giggled as Ticktock continued to push and playfully ram against her. Without a second thought, Poppy reached out, put her arms around the wiggly goat, and buried her face into Ticktock's bristly coat.

"I love you, Ticktock," she whispered.

I'll never let anyone hurt you, she promised silently.

A little later Claire brought a pillow and blanket out to the goat barn. "Don't worry. No one saw me, nor do they know you're out here." She softened the fresh hay and covered Poppy with the quilt. "After tonight I'll find you a safe place to stay," she promised. "But for now you'll be fine right here."

"Why are you bein' so nice to me?" Poppy asked. "Your pa knows I'm not . . . a good girl."

"Deep inside, you *are* a good girl, Poppy. You're a jewel."

Poppy bowed her head. "Ma told me I was a good girl when I stole things for her."

"No one ever explained to you that stealing is wrong, Poppy. You never knew that you hurt people when you steal from them."

"I didn't want to hurt anyone."

"Of course you didn't," Claire said. "And that tells me that you're a good girl. And now that you know it's wrong, you can stop stealing. I'll help you, Poppy. I promise." Claire gave Poppy a kiss on the cheek. "Good night, dear."

"Good night, Miss Claire," Poppy said.

"Just call me Claire. After all, we're best friends, aren't we?"

Poppy nodded and snuggled under the blanket.

After Claire tiptoed back to the house, Poppy called softly to the goat. "Come here with me, Ticktock. I don't want to be alone."

Ticktock came into the little barn and curled up on the floor next to the bed of hay where Poppy was lying. No more stealing? It was a scary thought. How else could she live? *I didn't think I was hurting anyone when I stole. It just didn't matter. But now that I almost have a family . . . now it does matter.* She sighed, turned her cheek to the cool, sweet-smelling pillow, and closed her eyes.

It was still dark when Poppy heard Ticktock's bell ringing loudly and then felt someone shaking her. She sat up and squinted in the darkness.

Sheila was sitting on the hay. "Ma's had me watchin' you, Poppy. I even saw you eatin' dinner at the Butterworths'." She laughed. "You sat right at their fancy table . . . but I see they kicked ya out here to the goat barn rather than let ya sleep in their house."

"Why are you here? Ma said I had till Friday to get the key."

"I know. She wants ya to come to Conley's Patch in the mornin'. If ya don't show up, she'll come and getcha herself—and you can say good-bye to that little beast of a goat. Ma's got plans for that animal." Sheila pulled the blanket off Poppy. "It'll be light soon, so ya better come with me now."

"But I don't wanna, Sheila. I wanna stay here—even if I do sleep in a goat barn. It's better than sleeping on that dirt floor with the noise and the dog fightin' and yellin' that goes on all night."

"Listen, just do what Ma wants. Get her a key to the jewelry store and then you can leave and do whatever ya wants. She just needs the key so's they can rob the store without any noise or trouble." She yanked Poppy by the arm. "Get up *now*!"

"No!" Poppy pulled away. "I'm not going with you."

Sheila put her face close to Poppy's. "All right, then I'll bring the goat instead." The dawn was brightening now and Poppy realized that Sheila had a rope in her hand. "I brought this so I can lead your *friend* here back to Ma's. The dogs in the pits might like to make mincemeat out of this goat."

The pits! Where dogs fight other dogs or animals viciously? Where every night she heard the dogs yelping in pain as the gamblers cheered them on, usually to their death? No! She'd never let that happen to Ticktock.

"Don't you touch this goat!" Poppy yelled, then put her hand over her mouth. "I'll come with you, Sheila, but *please* leave the goat here," she said, lowering her voice.

"Come on, then." Sheila yanked Poppy by the hand, dragging her out of the paddock and down to the main street.

CHAPTER TWENTY-FOUR

- *Who's to Blame?* -

Justin had thought all night Tuesday about ways to pay the store—and Father—the difference between a silver chain and a fourteen-karat white-gold chain. He wondered how he could ever explain the mistake.

Still, he thought Charlie should have recognized that the watch chain was white gold instead of silver. He was the great jewelry designer and the king of salesmen, wasn't he?

There was no way around it. The fault was really Justin's. He had rushed to finish tagging the chains, and he had made the mistake. He'd have to own up to it and face the consequences.

When Justin walked through the jewelry store door that morning—school was off that day for teacher meetings—Charlie, who was behind a counter, put up both hands and shook his head.

"Father discovered the chain is missing," Charlie whispered. "He's upset, Justin."

"What did you tell him?"

"Nothing. It's up to *you* to explain what happened—not me. He wants to see you in his office right away."

Justin took a deep breath and headed to the back of the store, where his father was working on the books. He looked up when he saw Justin. "Did you know there's a chain missing? A fourteen-karat white-gold chain? Do you know where it is?"

Justin hesitated, trying to find a way to deflect the blame. "No, Father, I . . . don't know . . . Er . . . it was here yesterday when I tagged it." *If Father thinks it was stolen . . . well, he wouldn't blame me, would he? Sure, that's the way to go . . . just let Father think someone stole it.*

"Are you telling me someone came into the store and no one was around to keep an eye on things? Where were you?

Where was Charlie? This shop should never be open when there's no one to watch over the jewelry. Why, any street kid could come in here and steal—" Father suddenly stopped speaking and slammed a fist onto the worktable. "A street kid. Of course! It's that little thief you brought into our house—that Poppy. She's the one who stole that chain!"

At first Justin was speechless. Sure, Poppy was a street kid from Conley's Patch, but there was no reason to believe . . . "Oh, no, Father . . . Poppy wasn't even in the store—"

Father interrupted Justin. "Don't try to protect her, Justin. We both know who stole that watch chain. Don't we?"

"I don't think Poppy would . . ."

"Of course she would . . . and she did! Who else could it be? Poppy knows the store. You've had her in here before. Claire brings her into our house and gives her clothes and food! I said a wild thing like Poppy would bite the hand that feeds her, and she has! That's the thanks we get for being nice to that . . . street urchin!"

Charlie came into the room. "What's going on?"

"You go back out into the showroom right now," Father ordered, "before someone else comes in and robs us."

Charlie looked puzzled. "Father, if I have to leave the showroom, I always lock the front door. What do you mean, 'before someone else comes in and robs us'? Who's robbed us?"

"Who do you think? Poppy, of course." Father crossed his arms over his chest. "You know she was brought up in Conley's Patch. They teach them how to steal from the time they can walk."

Charlie's eyes darted to Justin. "Is that what Justin told you? That Poppy stole the chain?"

"No, but the chain was stolen—and who else was around here? Poppy! It's obvious."

"Er . . . I don't think Poppy was inside the store yesterday, was she, Ch-charlie?" Justin stammered.

"I only heard her out on the sidewalk with Claire," Charlie said. "Before that, I don't know."

"Apparently you weren't in the showroom all the time," Father said accusingly. "Or you'd have seen her." He turned to Justin. "Don't try to protect that girl. We all know who stole that chain. You've got to get it back, Justin. And Claire will need to know she must not let Poppy into our house again."

"But, Father," Justin began.

"Not another word," Father said. "Be glad I don't call the police this time. But if she ever steals from us again, I am calling the police." He walked out into the other room, leaving Charlie and Justin alone in the workshop.

"Why did you tell him the chain was stolen?" Charlie asked.

"I didn't. He just assumed it was stolen. He didn't give me a chance to explain what really happened," Justin whispered.

"You're willing to let him believe Poppy stole it?"

"We know she didn't take it, Charlie, but if Father thinks it was stolen, he won't blame us."

"It's not right to put the blame on Poppy."

"Well then, why don't you tell Father you didn't know the difference between sterling and white gold?" Justin challenged.

"I *did* know the difference. That's why I went in and checked the invoice list. But *you* don't know the difference between eight dollars and eighty dollars and *you* are the one who put the wrong price on the tag."

Justin felt a lump in his throat—the kind that came when he was about to cry. "If I tell Father what really happened, he'll think I'm stupid. He'll never let me work in the store again."

"I think the right thing to do is tell the truth. He will be mad, but it's better than lying."

"I'll tell him. Just give me some more time, Charlie. I want to figure out the best way—so he won't be too mad at me."

Charlie nodded curtly and left the room, leaving Justin alone with his fears.

CHAPTER TWENTY-FIVE

- The Key . . . or Else! -

Sheila opened the door to the underground room that had been Poppy's home for many years. Poppy cringed at the foul, musty stench. How could she stand going back after seeing shiny clean floors, lavender-smelling pillows, and sparkling dinnerware? Even Ticktock smelled like sweet hay.

"Here she is," Sheila announced to Ma, who was counting out coins on the table.

"Oh, it's our Poppy, who's come home again. We missed you, dearie." Ma's gaze shifted down over the dress

Poppy wore. "Oh, you're wearing that dress that caused all the trouble. Hmm. I thought I gave it to Renee." Ma got up and strode toward Poppy. She smiled, but her eyes were dark slits.

Poppy knew that look and froze with fear. Her knees felt weak. Would Ma slap her around? Poppy vowed not to argue or make a scene. She'd be Poppy the pickpocket and pretend to do everything Ma wanted.

And then she'd run away from Chicago. She'd always wanted to stow away on a big steamer and go somewhere else. But what would happen to Ticktock?

"Noreen, go upstairs to the tavern and get Mr. Plant down here," Ma ordered. "He wants to talk to Poppy."

Noreen, who was sprawled on one of the mattresses, got up quickly and went out the door, but not before she sent a warning look to Poppy and mouthed the words *Watch out!*

Mr. Plant! He owned the place and allowed all sorts of mobsters, thieves, runaway criminals, and gamblers to live there and do jobs for him. *Why does he want to talk with me?* Poppy wondered. She took a deep breath and tried to still her shaking hands.

Already she could hear the clomp of footsteps, and

then Mr. Plant himself entered Ma's room, a big smile on his round face. He was much shorter than Noreen and looked like a jolly gnome. However, everyone at the Willow knew how powerful and important he was in Conley's Patch.

"Well, well, Poppy," he said in his highfalutin British accent. "I hear you are friends with the Butterworth jewelry family. Moving up in the world, eh?"

Poppy just stood there, not knowing how to reply. Ma Brennan, who was next to Poppy, nudged her sharply with her elbow. "Where are your manners? Answer Mr. Plant," she snapped.

"Yes, I know the Butterworths a little."

"A little!" Ma jeered. "You're practically livin' with them! Sheila watched you through the window last night, setting the table with real silver."

"Sure, now, you took a spoon or fork." Mr. Plant winked at Poppy and held out his hand. "Hand it over, child."

"No!" Poppy answered angrily. "I didn't take anything."

Moans came from Sheila and Noreen. "You ain't got the brains you were born with," Noreen taunted.

"Just wait until Julia and Renee come back from the streets," Sheila put in. "They'll never believe you had a chance like that and didn't take it."

"All that expert training I gave you is wasted." Ma looked at Mr. Plant apologetically. "Ain't it a shame? You bring up children, teach 'em all you know, and they turn around and fail ya."

Mr. Plant shook his head sadly. "Your mother here brought you up like her own flesh and blood—ever since you was a little one. She sacrificed a lot to take you in."

"I treated her like my very own child," Ma whined. "Now all I ask of her is to get us a key to the jewelry store, and she won't even do that for me."

"But, Ma," Poppy said, "once you get into the jewelry store, you still have to open the safe."

"Oh, we can take care of a safe easy enough," Mr. Plant said.

"After all I've done for you, Poppy, the least you can do—," Ma began.

"Hush, Mary." Mr. Plant used Ma's first name as if they were related. "Poppy will help us, won't you, dear?"

"What will you do if I get the key?" Poppy asked.

"We'll go in and take a few pieces of the fine jewelry,"

Mr. Plant said. "You'll make it easy for us so no one will get hurt."

"It's only right to do this job for us. You owe it to *me*." Ma pushed her face close to Poppy's. *"Understand?"*

Mr. Plant put his arm around Poppy's shoulder. "Poppy, look at it this way. You're not being disloyal to the Butterworths. If you don't help us, you'll be disloyal to *us*—those who've taken care of you all these years. We're not bad people. We're hardworking, and we use our skills and brains to get what should rightly belong to us."

"'Us'?" Ma scowled. "This is *my* show! Robbing the Butterworths is all my idea."

"You can't do this by yourself, Mary," Mr. Plant said kindly. "And since we'll be working with some of my best safecrackers, we'll *all* benefit from Poppy's help by splitting the profits." He turned once again to Poppy. "Now, I understand that your friend, that Butterworth boy, has a little goat. I'm sure it's a charming little thing."

Poppy stood as still as a soldier. She knew what was coming now. They knew she loved Ticktock and they'd use the little goat as a means to get the key.

Mr. Plant spoke in a quiet, ominous voice. "You do not want anything to happen to that sweet little nanny, do you? Of course not. We promise you that she's going to be just fine—as long as *you* do this one little simple thing for *us*. That's fair enough. Right?"

Poppy nodded.

"All right, child," he said with a leering smile. "I want you to bring the key to us by Friday. That gives you two more days. You're a clever girl who will have no trouble getting a simple thing like a key."

"Off you go," Ma said. "By Friday at suppertime. No later, or that little goat will be served up in a pot of stew."

Poppy ran out the door and up the steps to the dusty street. The wind was blowing hard and dirt slapped against her face.

If only there was a way out of this! No matter what I do, the Butterworths will be hurt.

WEDNESDAY NIGHT,
OCTOBER 4, 1871

CHAPTER TWENTY-SIX

- *Father Lays Down the Law* -

"Are you feeling well, Justin?" Mother asked. "You've hardly eaten a bite tonight."

"I'm just . . . tired," Justin replied. He didn't know himself why he wasn't hungry. The pressure was off him about that gold chain. Father had it all figured out that Poppy was to blame. *I hope she doesn't show up around here,* he thought. *Father would be furious, and Poppy wouldn't even know why.* He felt sick to his stomach and pushed his plate away.

"I don't believe the smoke from the fires is healthy,"

Claire said. "We've been breathing in smoke day after day."

"That's true," Father agreed. "A leather plant down by the river caught on fire today. What a stink that made." He cut a large chunk of pot roast from the platter and put it onto his plate.

"The meat is perfect," Claire said. "I hope I will be as good a cook as you when I get married, Mother."

"It's been simmering all day on the stove. That's why it's so tender," Mother said. "But it's made the kitchen so hot. Maybe we should have eaten in the dining room, where it's cooler."

"It *is* hot in here," Charlie said, getting up. "I'll open the back door for a few minutes. The cool air will feel good."

"There are dozens of fires all over the city," Father said. "The fire alarms and engines are everywhere. The noise is dreadful."

"The firemen are exhausted," Claire said. "Forrest thinks he'll open the church for refreshments for them soon."

"That would be nice," Mother said, nodding. "Forrest is conscious of people's needs. He's a good man, Claire."

"He's a lucky man to get a girl like our Claire." Father helped himself to a slice of bread. "But you are too extreme with your kindness, Claire."

Claire put down her fork and looked at her father questioningly. "How can I be too extreme with kindness?"

"It's that girl, Poppy," Father explained. "Didn't the boys tell you how she stole a valuable watch chain from the store?"

"No." Claire glanced at her brothers. "When did this happen?"

"Er . . . we don't know exactly *when*," Justin said. "And we're not really sure it was her. I mean . . ."

"If you're not sure, then don't blame her." Claire's voice rose and she shook her finger at the boys. "Just because she's had to grow up without real parents, in a horrible place, does not mean she's stolen that chain. You're *assuming* it was she who did it."

"It's a valid conclusion," Father stated emphatically. "She's a thief, she's been in our store several times, and the chain is missing. I don't need any more proof than that."

"Oh, Father," Charlie said nervously. "She's been in the store only once."

"You admit you're not always at the front of the store," Father said accusingly.

"See, Father? You *are* assuming it was poor little Poppy." Claire's voice shook as she stood up and carried her plate to the sink.

"Face reality, my child. Next thing you'll be inviting Poppy to live with us. She'd steal everything we have right from under our noses."

"I don't believe she stole that chain," Claire insisted.

"She was born and bred to be a thief," Father said, crossing his arms over his chest. "Do not trust her. I do not want her in this house again. That's an order. Do you all understand?"

"Yes, Father," Claire said wearily as the others murmured their compliance. She walked to the open door and stood there, looking out into the darkness.

CHAPTER TWENTY-SEVEN

- *False Accusations* -

Poppy spent the rest of the day down by the ships, watching the powerful waves that swept up against the shore. It was pleasant down here on the shoreline of Lake Michigan, where the smell of smoke was blown away by the strong breeze. All day the fire engines rushed around the city and the ringing of their bells carried over the wind. Spirals of smoke from brush fires looked like witches' fingers poking the sky.

The *Highland* steamer was tied with huge ropes up to a wharf near Poppy. It was such a big boat that it hardly moved against the wind and surf.

If I could hide away on that ship, I would. Then I wouldn't have to have that stinkin' key made for Ma. But if I don't show up with the key, they'll go after Ticktock.

Poppy could only imagine how sad Justin would be. He loved that little goat and was so excited when he'd brought her to the store to show Poppy. He'd even built that neat goat barn for her. It hurt Poppy to think how Justin might feel. She'd feel the same way, because she loved Ticktock, too.

I guess that's what happens when you love someone, she reflected. *You'd do anything to protect them. And then you always get hurt. I can't think of anyone who'd protect me or even care if something bad happened. Maybe Justin would . . . Claire would, I think.*

What shall I do? If I tell Claire what's happened and how Mr. Plant and Ma are planning to rob the store, maybe she'd know what to do. But if the police came and caught Ma or Mr. Plant's safecrackers, everyone back at the Willow would know I told . . . and they'd come after me.

Poppy stood up and headed away from the waterfront. She'd go see Claire and ask her what she'd do if someone she loved was in danger.

The sun was setting. By the time she'd get to Justin's

house, it would be dark. She'd sneak into the goat house. Claire would surely suspect she was there and go out to see her. Hadn't she said she had an idea for a place where Poppy could stay? Poppy walked faster. Up the streets and away from the water, the smell of smoke was strong. The wind blew circles of dried leaves around her feet.

She reached the Butterworths' house and went directly to the goat's paddock. She was about to open the gate when the kitchen door opened. She could see Charlie silhouetted against the light. "The cool air will feel good," he said to someone inside.

Poppy could see the family seated around the large oak table. She longed to be with them. Yet Mr. Butterworth had made it clear she wasn't welcome. But why? She had never stolen anything from *them*. Well, of course, she *had* made an impression of the key to the shop—but that was before she got to know the family. And no one knew she had done that.

I wonder what they're talking about. Maybe Mr. Butterworth has changed his mind about me.

She slipped closer to the house, crouched behind a bush, and strained to hear the voices inside. They were talking about Pastor Belmont and the church. It was hard to hear over the wind. But then she heard Mr. Butterworth yell her name loudly.

"It's that girl, Poppy!" he exclaimed. "Didn't the boys tell you how she stole a valuable watch chain from the store?"

Poppy gasped. *I never stole anything from the store! What are they talking about?* Instinctively she felt like running in and defending herself, but she didn't want them to know she was sneaking around, listening from the bushes. Perhaps she had heard wrong. She climbed under the rail and crept onto the porch—closer to the open door.

"Next thing you'll be inviting Poppy to live with us!" Mr. Butterworth was saying. "She'd steal everything we have right from under our noses."

Claire was speaking now, but it was hard to hear. "I . . . believe she stole . . . chain."

Oh, no, you can't believe it, Claire. I would never take anything from you or your family.

How could they say such things? The one time in Poppy's life that she cared about doing the right thing . . . and they think she stole something. A lump gathered in her throat.

Mr. Butterworth was yelling again. "I do not want

her in this house again. That's an order. Do you all understand?"

There was some murmurs, but when she heard Claire say, "Yes, Father," Poppy felt a stab in her heart.

She forgot about the sounds of her own footsteps as she ran off the porch, but she didn't care if they knew she'd been listening.

"That's what I get for believing I could be part of a real family!" she muttered, trying hard not to let the tears come. "I musta been crazy! Well, I'm going to give Ma the key so they won't hurt Ticktock. Then I'm stowing away on the *Highland*. I never wants to see any of them Butterworths again. Never!"

WEDNESDAY NIGHT,
OCTOBER 4, 1871

CHAPTER TWENTY-EIGHT

- *Confessions* -

"Did you hear footsteps on the porch?" Justin asked.

"Yes, it sounded like someone running," Charlie replied, getting up.

Claire went onto the porch. "There's someone . . . a small shadow . . . Oh, it looks like Poppy! She's running down the driveway to the street." Claire gasped. "She must have heard our whole conversation. All the blame everyone was putting on her . . . oh, the poor child."

Justin felt as though his heart had hit the floor. Poppy knew she was being blamed for something she didn't do. He had only hoped what happened to the gold chain would just blow over and Father would forget about it. He really didn't want to blame Poppy—he just . . . He looked at Charlie, who was sending messages with his eyes and shaking his head.

It was time to tell Father what had really happened. "Father . . . ," Justin began.

But Father was still talking. "It's just as well Poppy knows we don't want thieves around here," he was saying. "We trusted her . . ."

"No, you didn't, Father," Claire admonished. "You never welcomed her or gave her a chance."

"That's right. I'm not welcoming a little guttersnipe from Conley's Patch into our house or into our jewelry shop. You placed temptation in front of her, Claire."

"I do not believe she stole anything from us," Claire protested. "Why, she had a chance to steal silverware or other things when she was here, but nothing is missing. I think she was just beginning to know what love and affection are. . . . She never—"

"Love and affection?" Father exclaimed. "She stole from the store. That's how she shows her love and affection."

"Your father is right, dear," Mother said. "If she stole from us—after the kindness you've shown her—then I'd just let her go."

"Father, I need to tell you something," Justin said.

"Not now, Justin." Father cut himself a piece of pie for dessert. "In fact, I don't want that girl's name ever mentioned in this house again."

Justin felt as if something were about to explode inside of him. "Poppy never stole the chain!" he blurted out. "I marked the price wrong and I didn't know how to tell you. It was all *my* fault. Poppy had nothing to do with it."

Silence. No one spoke, but everyone turned and stared at Justin.

"Did you hear me? I said it was *my* fault." Justin buried his face in his hands. "I was going to tell you, but I was scared. I was afraid you'd think I was too stupid to ever work in the store—or cut a gemstone—or . . . ever be trusted." He could feel the wetness from the tears on his cheeks.

Another loud silence. Justin peeked out from between his hands. Father was frozen with a fork halfway to his mouth. Mother's face looked as if she had been struck.

Finally Claire spoke up, her voice shaking. "I just

knew Poppy wouldn't betray us." She looked at her father accusingly. "She needed our love, not our distrust and suspicion."

"It was only natural to blame her, with her background, her life at the Willow," Father argued defensively. "But I would have never suspected Justin of lying or accusing an innocent person."

"Nor would I." Mother shook her head sadly.

"Honestly, I didn't dream you'd blame Poppy. I was hoping it would all blow over and be forgotten," Justin said.

"No one stole the watch chain," Charlie said. "It was the only white-gold chain in the batch. The rest were silver, and Justin couldn't tell the difference. He marked the tag as silver, not gold, and we sold it as silver."

"Then you're to blame, too," Father said accusingly.

"I didn't think to check it until the customer paid me," Charlie admitted. "Then I went and looked at the inventory list and realized it was gold. The customer wouldn't give it back or pay the difference."

"And you've got to agree that it would be easy to mix up eight dollars and eighty dollars," Justin interrupted. "Anyone could make that mistake."

Mother shook her head. "I'm shocked at the two of you!"

"Yes, we're disappointed in you both," Father agreed. "Surprisingly, I'm more upset about your blaming Poppy than for selling the chain as silver. I feel bad that you couldn't tell me the truth."

"I was about to tell you." Charlie's shoulders slumped dejectedly. "I'm really sorry, but I promised Justin I'd give him the chance to explain first."

"Father, I don't like to say this to you," Claire said, "but you are just as guilty. You had Poppy tried and convicted without even letting her explain—and just when she was learning to trust . . ." Claire pulled on the sweater that was draped over her chair. "I'm going out to find her." She pointed her finger at Justin and Charlie. "And you two are going to bend over backward to make it up to her."

"Where are you going at this hour?" Mother asked. "It's dangerous out in Poppy's neighborhood. You can't go there alone."

"These boys are coming with me." By Claire's firm lips and stature, Justin knew nothing would stop her from trying to make things right—if it wasn't too late.

CHAPTER TWENTY-NINE

- It Was All a Big Lie! -

Poppy once again found herself at the lakeside. She found a grassy spot near the shore where she curled up, her knees drawn to her chest, and pulled her sweater around her. The wind must have switched, because the smell of smoke was strong and the stars were dim.

Poppy decided she'd run away just as soon as she gave the wax impression of the key to Ma. She'd never come back to this stinking place, and she'd never trust anyone again. She'd take care of herself and . . . if she had to steal to eat, that's what she'd do. But now it would be for herself, not for people like Ma and Mr. Plant, who used her to steal for them.

She thought of Justin and Claire. She'd get rid of any stupid idea that she could be part of a family. She pushed the Butterworths out of her mind—for good, she hoped, because it hurt to remember Claire, the new dress, the pretty rooms, and the candlelight on the silverware.

There was no way she could ever be different. How could she? She had no family, no chance to go to school and learn to read. There was no one who'd give a chance to someone like her.

She closed her eyes and wondered if Ticktock missed her. Ticktock seemed to love Poppy, and Ticktock didn't care if she was a thief. The goat ran to greet her, the little bell around her neck jingling and her tail wagging, whenever Poppy visited.

Well, tomorrow Poppy would give the wax key impression to Ma. Then at least Ticktock would be safe.

Poppy looked up at the starlit sky and remembered the wishes she'd made. *Wishes don't come true! You'd have to be really stupid to believe that.*

And what did Claire say about me that night when she gave me the dress? That I'm like one of those rocks—the geode—and that I have a sparkling crystal of goodness deep inside of me?

What good is it? I'm still Poppy the pickpocket, and everything she said is all a big lie.

Poppy's eyes were heavy, and soon she fell asleep to the sound of the water lapping against the shore.

THURSDAY MORNING,
OCTOBER 5, 1871

CHAPTER THIRTY

- The Search Begins -

Justin groaned when the sun filtered through the cur-
tains in his bedroom. It couldn't be morning already. It
seemed as if he'd just gone to bed. He'd been up late with
his brother and sister, combing the streets for Poppy.

It was scary out at Conley's Patch in the daylight,
but in the dark it was terrifying. No wonder Father and
Mother had put up such a fuss when Claire insisted she'd
go look for Poppy right away.

They had searched streets and alleys as far as the
Willow, where Poppy lived. They debated whether or

not to go inside and ask about Poppy. But the place was noisy and rowdy with wild singing and yelling. "We can't go in there. All kinds of peculiar people come out of their holes at night," Charlie said softly. "And they stay out until dawn."

"Then they go back into their holes," Claire said.

It seemed as if Claire would never grow weary of searching for Poppy. "I've *got* to find her and tell her we know she didn't steal from us."

But when Justin finally said, "Poppy knows her way around here better than we do. We'll never find her. And it's not safe to speak with any of these roughs, so we can't ask anyone around here," even Claire agreed.

At that moment, somewhere inside the Willow, cheers erupted while dogs snarled and yelped as if in pain.

"They've got dog pits and gambling here," Charlie said. "Let's get out of this rotten place, quick!"

And so they left the area and returned home as fast as they could.

It took Justin a long time to get to sleep. All he could think of was Poppy and how he had let the blame fall on her. *Why did I do this? Why didn't I confess to my own mistake instead of making this a hundred times worse?*

Now, he turned over and punched his pillow. At least he had a pillow. Poppy was probably sleeping on a sidewalk somewhere. He suspected she didn't want to go back to the Willow.

She had once talked about running away on a ship. Justin decided he wouldn't go to school today. Instead, he'd go down by the river docks and search for her.

Mother will never let me miss a day of school to search for Poppy, especially when we had a day off yesterday. So I'll play hooky. That's what I'll do.

Justin dressed for school and headed to the kitchen, where Mother was reading the newspaper. He put a slice of bacon on his toast and gulped it down with fresh cider from a neighbor's farm.

"How did you sleep, dear?" Mother asked. "You went to bed so late last night."

"Didn't sleep much. I'm too worried about Poppy."

"Oh, that child is out of our lives, dear. You'll never see her again. But this is a lesson that you'll remember all your life."

Justin put on his jacket. "I'm going to feed Ticktock now, Mother, and then I'll go on to school." He hated to lie, but he had to find Poppy.

Justin went to the goat barn, where Ticktock was waiting. "Hi, my little nanny," Justin whispered as he brushed his pet with the wire brush. Ticktock leaned into the brush with her head and snuffled loudly. Then Justin put fresh water and food into the feeders and thought of Poppy again. Ticktock had love and care. Poppy had nothing. She slept in this goat barn, and it was better than any place she had ever called home.

He had to find her.

CHAPTER THIRTY-ONE

- *Poppy's Decision* -

On Thursday morning, Poppy awoke to the sound of waves, boat whistles, and voices. The sky was light but clouded with smoke. She had only today and tomorrow to give Ma and Mr. Plant the wax impression of the key. Then she'd sneak on board one of the ships and sail away to somewhere else.

Yes, that's what she'd do. After all, the Butterworths had never really cared about her. Even Claire said she believed Poppy had taken . . . something. Well, the Butterworths be danged. She'd had enough of them!

She got up, adjusted her sweater, and headed to a nearby park. There, at a small beach, she washed her face in the water.

"Whatcha doin', kid?" A man dressed in raggedy clothes staggered up to Poppy. "Got any food?"

"No!" She turned away. Although she was a street person herself, especially now that she had nowhere to live, she knew she had to be wary of beggars who killed for just a bite of food.

She was hungry, too, but she wouldn't allow herself to think about food right now. She had to take the wax impression she had made of Mr. Butterworth's key to Ma Brennan straightaway.

As she headed up the dusty road, she stopped suddenly. Was that Justin coming down the street? For an instant she wanted to run toward him and call his name. Then she recalled the accusations the Butterworths had made about her. She'd vowed never to see them or speak with any of them again. She ducked into the next alley and ran around trash and garbage to the next street. Then she suddenly realized that the boy could not have been Justin. He'd be in school at this hour of the morning.

There was no one around the empty lot where the

wax impression was hidden. Once again Poppy found the loose stone and reached inside the cavity. She pulled out the small matchbox and the four dollars that were left. Yes, everything was exactly as she had left it.

Poppy would need the money now that she had decided to stow away on the *Highland*. It wasn't going to last long, but at least it was something.

She stuffed the money and the little box containing the wax into her pocket and replaced the stone. She'd probably never come back to this place. She'd be far away in a few days. Her heart skipped a beat at the thought of what lay ahead. At the same time, she was scared. Who would have anything to do with a girl her age who had no family or friends? Perhaps she could clean houses—become a maid. That wouldn't be bad. Maybe the people in the household would learn to love her . . . like she thought Claire had.

Poppy didn't want to think about Claire, but all the sweet things that Justin's sister had said and promised came back like the smoke on the wind and then disappeared in the sky.

Tears welled up again. *Only stupid people let their hearts believe anything,* she decided. Poppy took out the box of wax, opened it, and studied the impression of the key to the jewelry store. It was a perfect cast. Ma would have no trouble making a key from it.

Still, Claire told Poppy she was learning to love her. And Poppy had felt like Mew must feel—warm and loved, tucked away in a safe place next to Claire's heart.

A safe place. That feeling of belonging was gone now, but at least, for once in her whole life, she had felt part of a family—part of a friendship—in a safe place. That was something, wasn't it? Something to remember—the rest of her life.

She took the wax impression out of the box and held it in her hand. Then, with a sudden decision, she threw it to the ground and stomped on it hard.

CHAPTER THIRTY-TWO

- Gentleman's Agreement -

Justin walked the same streets they had the night before. Where had Poppy gone? Back to that awful place where she'd lived? He hoped not.

Justin tried to take in everything—every shadow, corner, alley, and doorway. But Poppy seemed to have vanished off the earth. *Please, God, let Poppy be all right.*

Suddenly his eyes fell upon a girl at the end of the street. *It's Poppy!* She looked up at him and it seemed as if she was about to call to him. But then she ducked into an alley and disappeared.

"Stop! Poppy!" Justin flew down the street, raced into the alley, and threw aside the many crates, boxes, and trash cans that were strewn haphazardly everywhere. "Poppy!" he yelled.

She was not there.

I'll go down to the wharves by the lake, which was my original plan. Since she wanted to run away on a steamer, I'll check every boat that's hitched up by the lake and then I'll check the river.

On the way to the lake, he passed a park where a few mothers were walking their children in prams. One vagrant stumbled around picking up trash and looking in rubbish bins.

Justin headed toward the grubby hobo, who seemed to be searching for food. "Have you seen a girl, about twelve, who might have spent the night on the streets around here?"

"Hmm," said the man. "I saw one little girl. She seemed younger than twelve, though. She had no food, so I walked away."

"Poppy looks younger than twelve. Where did she go?"

"Up the street over there." The man put on a pitiful face. "Hey, sonny, ain't you got any money or food for me? Be a kind boy. I'm real hungry."

"Sorry," Justin said, and ran across the road and up the hill. "I think that was Poppy I saw earlier," he said to himself. "But where would she go from here?"

He was about to head back when he stopped in his tracks. Patrick Cahill and Four Fingers Foley were running toward him. "Hey, Rotten!" Patrick called. "We warned ya we'd get ya if you showed up in our territory."

Justin wanted to run, but he thought maybe these thugs would know where Poppy was. Still, would they tell him? "I'm not bothering anyone," Justin said as the boys came close.

"You're botherin' *us*," Fingers said with a sneer. "And we're goin' to teach you a lesson you'll never forget."

Justin turned to run, but it was too late. Fingers caught him by his jacket and pulled him back. Then he punched Justin in the gut.

Panic and the blow to the stomach were too much, and Justin's breakfast came up in a gush. He threw up— right in Fingers's face and all over his pullover sweater.

"Yuck!" Fingers screamed, backing away.

Patrick stopped his forward pursuit of Justin and backed up cautiously. But then, seeing Fingers covered with vomit, he doubled over, laughing.

"It ain't funny!" Fingers yelled, looking down at the stinking mess. He began to pull the sweater over his head, but now his face was buried in the vomit. He yanked the sweater back down again, and then, as his head emerged, now covered with even more slop, he heaved a gushing fountain of his own breakfast out of his mouth—this time all over Patrick!

All three boys stared down at their soggy, smelly clothes. Then they looked up at one another. Justin, who was about to run away, started to laugh.

"You are a hog," Fingers said to his chum, Patrick. "I should take ya to the slaughterhouse."

"You are a stinkin' rotten swine yourself," Patrick hollered.

Justin said, "I'm not walking all the way home in this stink." He took off his jacket and threw it into a nearby rubbish bin.

Patrick did the same. Fingers took a pocketknife out of his pants and cut away at the sweater. "This was my best sweater," he moaned.

"You mean it was your *only* sweater," Patrick said.

Fingers turned to Justin. "It's all your fault!"

"Well, I hope you've learned not to punch me in the

stomach," Justin replied. Then he added, "If you guys need sweaters or jackets, come on down to the Methodist church on Wabash Saturday morning. There'll be a load of good clothes there—free."

"We don't need any help from you!" Fingers said.

"If you find another sweater, you won't have to explain what happened to that one," Justin said.

"I told you, we don't need charity from you!" Fingers said in a saintly voice.

"Oh, forget it, then," Justin replied, turning to walk away.

"So why are you down here—and on a school day, too?" Fingers asked.

"I'm looking for Poppy."

"Poppy? Everyone's lookin' for her," Patrick told him.

"Like who?" Justin asked.

"Like Ma Brennan," Patrick answered. "Poppy was real stupid to run away from Ma. Now she's in real big trouble."

"Serves her right. No one dares to run away from Ma," Fingers added.

"Listen," Justin said, "if you see Poppy, tell her to come to my house right away. Let her know she's *not* in trouble with us. It's real important."

"Why should we do any favors for you?" Patrick asked. "What's in it for us?"

"I'll see that you get a new sweater and shirt at the church fair. That way you won't get in trouble with your mothers. How about it?"

Patrick was silent for a moment, thinking. Then he said, "We'll tell Poppy if and when we see her."

"Be sure you live up to your end of the deal," Fingers said. "A sweater for me and a shirt for Patrick."

"Methodist church. Wabash Avenue. Saturday morning," Justin said. "Bring Poppy, if you can."

THURSDAY MORNING,
OCTOBER 5, 1871

CHAPTER THIRTY-THREE

- Scary Plans -

Poppy looked down at the smashed and broken wax on the ground. *Now you've done it!* she thought. She'd destroyed the key and she'd have to answer to Ma and Mr. Plant. But worse, Ticktock was in real danger.

What could she do to save Ticktock? Ma said that Poppy had to give her the key to the jewelry store by Friday night or Ma would go after the goat. There was only one thing to do. Poppy would steal Ticktock from the Butterworths' and hide her. She'd find a place somewhere, somehow, where she and Ticktock would be safe.

Poppy spent the day in the small park, falling in and out of sleep on one of the benches. Now she was restless.

It was late afternoon and soon it would be dark. She was hungry, starving for something to eat. She wandered up the street to a little café near the park and went inside. A waitress looked her up and down. Poppy knew her pretty dress was now soiled and becoming tattered, but it was all she had to wear.

Poppy sat at the counter and ordered one cup of chicken soup for ten cents. She was happy to see that it was served with a plate of crackers. When no one was looking, she stuffed all the crackers into her pocket. Then she downed the soup slowly, enjoying every bite of chicken and carrot and potato. It was so good, she wished she'd ordered a whole bowl, but she knew she had to use her money carefully. Before she finished, she beckoned to the lady behind the counter. "Could I have a few more crackers, please?"

"I sure hope you have money to pay for this," the waitress said with a scowl as she slapped more crackers onto the plate.

"Course I do!" Poppy snapped. "But those crackers come with the soup, don't they?"

"Yes . . . but your soup is gone." The waitress took a long look at Poppy. "Well, you look like you need more crackers. There'll be no extra charge this time."

After Poppy paid, she went to the restroom, where she washed up. She again wished she had a comb, but since she didn't, she wet her hair and braided it, tying the bottoms with knots to keep the braids from falling apart.

It was dusk when she left the restaurant and started up the sidewalk toward the Butterworths' house. It would be dark by the time she got there. A wheezing steam fire engine pulled by two horses raced by, heading toward a glow in the distance—another fire. Sparks and cinders from the smoking chimney on the truck flew through the air. *I would think the smoke from the engines could start even more fires,* Poppy mused.

When she arrived at the Butterworths' house, lights in the windows showed the family was up and about inside. Perhaps Justin would be coming out to feed Ticktock. She'd wait until the lights went out before going down to the paddock and the goat barn. Justin would be broken-hearted when he found his goat was gone. He'd probably figure it was Poppy who'd taken her. He couldn't know she was trying to save his pet.

Poppy sat on a rock and waited until some of the lights had gone off. She then crept closer to the goat's enclosure. The cheery tinkling bell on Ticktock's collar jingled loudly as Poppy approached. Ticktock was waiting eagerly by the gate when Poppy went inside. "Oh, you sweet little thing," she whispered, opening her arms. The goat came closer to get hugged, and Poppy fed her one of the crackers from her pocket. "I do love you, Ticktock. I wish I could stay here forever with you, but it's not safe anymore."

She took off the collar with the bell and put on the old collar and leash that hung on the wall. "We have to be real quiet," she told the goat. "I have to hide you so Ma won't get you. That bell would give you away." She found some grain and stuffed it into the pail, then put the pail over her arm.

She led the goat out of the paddock and down the hill to the main road. Then she looked back at the quiet place she'd left. "I'm sorry, Justin," she murmured. "I wish I could explain why I have to do this. You think I'm a thief anyway. Now your heart will bust when you find your little goat is gone. You'll hate me for sure. But trust me—this is for the best."

Where would Poppy and Ticktock spend the night? She recalled a deserted shed near the docks. That's where she'd go, and as soon as she found a place on a ship, she and Ticktock would sail away.

CHAPTER THIRTY-FOUR

- *Ticktock Is Missing* -

Friday morning Justin went out to feed his goat. Ticktock was the only one who still loved him. Father and Mother were disappointed in him. Charlie was mad because everyone put some blame on him for allowing the gold watch chain to be sold as silver. Claire was sad and hardly spoke to anyone except Forrest and little Mew. The whole family was gloomy and grumpy. But Ticktock's little tail wagged and she bleated happily whenever she saw Justin.

So Justin was surprised that morning when he didn't hear the merry jingle of Ticktock's bell and when she didn't come out to greet him. "Ticktock!" he called. "Come here, little nanny." There was only silence. A cold dread swept over Justin as he tiptoed into the goat barn. It was empty! "Ticktock!" he yelled. "Where are you?"

Where could she be? Had she escaped from her enclosure somehow?

Justin looked around the barn. The pail was gone, and the grain bag was half empty. Ticktock's bell collar was hanging on the wall, but the old collar and leash were missing. Had Charlie or Claire taken Ticktock out of the stall? Justin ran back to the house, calling, "Claire! Charlie! Where is Ticktock?"

Charlie, Mother, and Father, who were all eating breakfast at the kitchen table, looked up in alarm. "Isn't she in her barn?" Charlie asked.

"No, and her leash and pail are gone—and some of her food, too." Justin ran to Claire's room. "Claire! Are you in there?"

The door opened and Claire peered out. "What's going on?" she asked sleepily.

"Ticktock is missing."

"Oh, no! Did she get out through the fence?"

"No! Someone took her."

"It was undoubtedly Poppy," Father called from the kitchen. "She took your goat to get even for your blaming her about the watch chain."

"Would she be that mean?" Justin asked as he came back to the table. His throat was tight and his eyes were about to overflow. "She knows how I love Ticktock." He slumped onto a chair, lowered his head onto the table, and buried his face in his arms. "I can't stand it. My poor little goat."

Claire came into the kitchen, dressed in a robe. "Poppy would never hurt Ticktock," she said.

"Why would she steal her?" Charlie asked.

"I told you why. She's getting even with us." Father sipped his coffee. "Another lesson in trusting scalawags."

"Father, someday you will be sorry for saying unkind things like that," Claire warned. "If we could find Poppy and talk with her, we'd know a lot about what's happening. I can't believe she'd do something so spiteful."

Justin looked up at his parents. "I *have* to find Ticktock. Please let me stay home from school today. Please!"

"We can't just take a day off whenever a problem arises," Father stated. "And you cannot stay home from school to look for a goat."

Justin looked away. *If Father ever knew I played hooky yesterday* . . .

Claire spoke up. "Father, you can see how upset Justin is. He loves that goat. If he goes to school today, I'm sure he won't be learning much when he's so worried about Ticktock."

Justin glanced at Claire gratefully. "You did tell me that Ticktock would be my responsibility, Father."

Father's face was stony cold. "No." He slammed his cup down with a bang, and coffee spilled onto the tablecloth.

"I'd say this is a *family emergency*," Mother insisted. "When there's an emergency, everyone should pitch in and lend a hand." She touched Father's shoulder. "You could help, too, dear. You know all the policemen in town. Why don't you go down to the police station? They might know something."

"I'll take care of the store," Charlie offered. "You'll have more success with the police, Father. They respect you."

There was a long silence in the room. Then Father spoke up. "Well, I guess it does make sense for Justin to look for his goat since he can't concentrate on his school-work while Ticktock is missing." He wiped his mouth with a napkin. "I suppose I can help, too, down at the police station."

"Thank you, dear," Mother whispered.

"Charlie, we won't open the store today. We'll all look for Ticktock." Father got up from his chair. "After I go to the police, I'll check the riverfront down by the wharves. Charlie, you and Justin go down to the lakeside."

"We already made plans to work at the church all weekend, distributing clothes to the poor. We'll ask everyone who comes in if they know Poppy and if they have any idea where she might be," Mother suggested.

Claire nodded eagerly. "Yes, there will be lots of people coming—especially on Saturday. Someone *must* have seen a girl with a goat."

"So you suspect Poppy, too," Father said pointedly.

Claire looked hard at her father. "Perhaps *someone* broke her heart enough to set her back into a life of crime."

"Perhaps *someone* did." Father looked away, his fingers tracing an embroidered leaf on the tablecloth. Then he sighed. "I know I share in the blame, too. Once we bring Ticktock home, maybe we can make things right with Poppy."

Claire reached out and took his hand. "And with one another," she added.

CHAPTER THIRTY-FIVE

- That's Just the Way It Is -

On Friday morning, Poppy opened the shed door and peeked out. Ticktock unfolded her legs and followed Poppy to the door.

The sun was bright and the fresh air smelled clean as a strong breeze blew across the waterfront. The lake shimmered like silver.

"We needs to find food for both of us and I needs a bathroom," Poppy said to Ticktock. "You greedy goat! Spillin' all the grain from the pail—and then eatin' it all up. Now there's not enough for today." At least there was some parched grass around for the goat to eat.

Poppy attached Ticktock's leash and walked toward a park with a privy and fresh water. She tied Ticktock to a tree while she went into the outhouse and then washed up at a public fountain.

"I sure wish I could take a swim or bathe somewhere. I feel so scummy," she told the goat. Ticktock looked up at her as if she understood. Poppy had two crackers left in her sweater pocket. She gave one to the goat, who snatched it quickly with her tongue. "If you eat slowly, like me, it will last longer," she told Ticktock. She counted the money in her pocket. Now she had four dollars and some change. She could get something to eat from a vendor with a cart, someone who sold fruit or hot dough. That way she wouldn't have to take her eyes off Ticktock.

It was time to think about stowing away on one of the steamers tied up nearby. It would be a big enough problem to get on board and hide herself—not to mention with a goat, too.

But she had to protect Ticktock. After tonight, Ma Brennan and Mr. Plant would be out to get them both.

As she started up the path toward the street, she saw

two boys heading her way. Oh, no! It was Four Fingers Foley and his pal, Patrick Cahill! She turned and headed in the opposite direction, but it was too late. "Hey, Poppy!" Fingers yelled. "Stop! I got a message for ya!"

Poppy started to run, but Ticktock, who was sniffing and gobbling food from an overturned garbage pail, pulled hard against her. And in one quick minute, the boys caught up with her.

"Leave us alone!" Poppy yanked frantically on the goat's leash.

"Aw, calm down. We ain't gonna hurt ya," Patrick said. "We got a message from your chum, Justin Butterworth."

A message from Justin? "What does he want?"

"I dunno. We saw him yesterday," Fingers told her. "He said to tell you he needs to see you right away."

"And to come to his house . . . or somethin'." Patrick scratched his head.

"Oh, sure! I'll do that. They'll throw me in jail," Poppy exclaimed. "They thinks I stole somethin' and I never did."

"Yeah? Then what are you doin' with his goat?" Fingers asked.

"Tryin' to save her. Ma Brennan's lookin' to kill her

'cause . . . well, never mind. It's none of your beeswax anyhow." Poppy bit her tongue. Would they tell Ma that they'd seen her with Ticktock?

"How come you two are such chums with Justin? You were always beatin' up on him," Poppy said.

"Well, he's not so bad." Fingers patted the goat. "He was lookin' everywhere for you. He said for you to go to his house."

"Ha! Not in a pig's eye!" Poppy started to walk away.

"We'll tell him what you said," Patrick promised. "We may see him at the Methodist church tomorrow. We're goin' to get new clothes."

Fingers snickered. "Justin threw up all over me when I punched him. Ruined my best sweater."

"Do you want us to tell him anything?" Patrick asked. "About the goat?"

Poppy thought about it for a few moments. "Yes. Tell him I took the goat to hide her from Ma Brennan. She said she'd make her into a stew or throw her into the dog pit. That's why I took her. Not to steal her." She put her hands on her hips. "Can you get that right?"

"We're not stupid," Fingers snapped. "Why would Ma Brennan give two hoots about that goat?"

"'Cause she's tryin' to get even with me for . . . oh, like I said, it's none of your beeswax!" She pulled Ticktock away and began walking toward the road.

"You ought to go to the church yourself with your messages. Then you can get some clothes. You're a mess, Poppy!" Fingers yelled after her.

Poppy could feel her face redden. Her pretty dress wasn't pretty anymore. She would never be one of the *nice* girls. But that's just the way it was.

SATURDAY MORNING,
OCTOBER 7, 1871

CHAPTER THIRTY-SIX

- Not in a Pig's Eye! -

Saturday morning was another sad day for Justin. This was the second day he went to the empty goat barn and sat on the doorsill. Everything was too quiet without Ticktock's bleating, her noisy bell, and the happy little sounds she usually made when she greeted him.

Although the family spent the better part of yesterday asking if anyone had seen a girl with a goat, no one had. Father even checked with the police, but not a soul had any idea where Poppy went with Ticktock.

They had eaten supper silently last night. Justin could

tell the rest of the family felt they'd done everything they could.

Later that Saturday morning, at the church fair, tables were filled with various items of clothing. One side of the hall had men's clothes—piles of sweaters, flannel shirts, trousers, and shoes, all only slightly worn. On hangers were nicely pressed suits and dress shirts. Justin was posted in that area, along with his chum Randy and Randy's father. Forrest was there, too, wandering among the people, inviting them to church services.

Claire and Mother helped on the other side of the hall, where women's and children's clothes were laid out in neat piles and on hangers.

All Justin could think of was Poppy and Ticktock. Poppy could use clothes. Maybe she'd come into the church today. But it wasn't likely. He knew she'd probably never show up around his family again. *In any case, she sure knew the best way to hurt me,* Justin thought. *She knows how much I love Ticktock. I'll never forgive her for stealing my goat.*

Justin's brooding was interrupted when he looked up to see Four Fingers Foley and Patrick Cahill enter the church hall. They looked uncomfortably out of place, treading slowly and uneasily into the large room. *Probably the first time they've been in a church,* Justin thought.

Justin went up to them. "I'll help you find a sweater and shirt as promised, fellas. Do you need anything else, Fingers?" he asked.

"Anything else that fits."

"I can use more new duds, too," Patrick added.

"But first, have you seen Poppy?" Justin asked.

"Yeah, yesterday—down by the park at the lake. We gave her your message, but she said she couldn't come to your house 'cause you'd probably have her arrested."

"Did she have Ticktock?"

"She sure did," Patrick answered. "She said she was protectin' your goat 'cause . . ." He turned to his pal. "Why had she taken Ticktock, Fingers?"

"You dummy. You can't remember your own name!" Fingers snapped. Then, turning to Justin, he said, "She said Ma Brennan was lookin' to steal Ticktock to kill her."

Patrick nodded. "Oh yeah—she said she'd cook her into a stew or throw her at the dogs."

"What?" Justin yelled, and several people, including Forrest, looked his way. "Why?" he asked more softly.

"I dunno. It was about Ma punishin' Poppy for somethin' or other," Patrick said.

"Yeah. Poppy said to tell you that she didn't steal Ticktock. She was hiding her from Ma."

"Why didn't she just come and tell me? Didn't you tell her we know she didn't steal anything?"

"She said she wouldn't come—not in a pig's eye. Those were her exact words," Fingers said.

"She may come here for clothes, though." Patrick looked accusingly at Fingers. "You told her she needed clothes and she looked a mess."

"I've got to talk to her. I thought she was getting even with me by stealin' my goat," Justin said. "So now it's time to come back and we can straighten everything out. It was all a big misunderstanding."

"It's more than that," Fingers said. "When Ma Brennan's out to get someone . . . believe you me, it's not just a *misunderstandin'*!"

"So Ticktock really is in danger, right?" Justin asked.

"Right," Fingers replied. "And I'm thinkin' Poppy's in big danger, too. Why don't you go lookin' down by the river park where we saw her?"

"She saw me Thursday. I called but she ran away.

Please, chums, if you see her first, tell her to come *here* to the church. She and Ticktock will be safe here."

"She won't come," Patrick said.

Fingers shook his head. "Nope. Not in a pig's eye."

CHAPTER THIRTY-SEVEN

- *Ticktock Goes to Church* -

Once again, this time on Sunday morning, Poppy opened the door of the deserted shed to a windy day—so windy, in fact, that the door almost pulled her outside when she released it. The sand and dust danced in swirls and circled over the dry streets and sidewalks. Wind gusted the surface of Lake Michigan in great waves and surf that cascaded over the shoreline. Boats tugged on their ropes, squealing and scraping against the posts and docks.

Poppy's stomach growled, begging for food. She didn't dare use the little money she still had—not yet, not until she safely stowed away aboard a ship heading for somewhere else.

Where would "somewhere else" be? Another city full of beggars and thieves, like Chicago?

It seemed as if the Butterworths hardly knew the Chicago where Poppy lived—the dark, underground, hidden places that disappeared in the morning sunlight as if they were only shadows or bad dreams.

On the other hand, the world of people like the Butterworths was a world Poppy hardly knew. That was a place where candles glistened and families laughed and loved. That would never be Poppy's world.

But Ticktock was from Justin's world, and it was time Poppy took her back. She would be in a safe place now that Fingers and Patrick had told Justin about Ma Brennan's threats. Thank goodness she had run into those two yesterday evening. Poppy was beginning to wonder how on earth she'd stow away on a ship with a goat.

I'll take her to the church and leave her there.

Poppy led the little goat up the road toward the Methodist church on Wabash Avenue. As they drew near, the church bells were ringing and families were passing through the heavy wooden doors. Were the

Butterworths there? Was Claire? When Claire married Pastor Belmont, she'd be living in the parish house next door. It was a big house—huge, in fact. Poppy smiled when she pictured little Mew roaming around the place. She missed holding that purring little furry bundle.

She went to the backyard of the parish house and hitched Ticktock to the end of a clothesline that had fallen to the ground. Perfect! The goat had room to roam and still couldn't get away from the yard. When Parson Belmont came home, he was sure to see—*and hear*—Ticktock, who would be bleating for attention.

Claire said there were sheep in the church. Well, now there's a goat, too.

"You'll be safe here, dearie." Poppy put her arms around Ticktock and pressed her face against the goat's stubbly neck. "Good-bye, Ticktock," she whispered. "I do love you."

Poppy turned away and headed back to the waterfront.

CHAPTER THIRTY-EIGHT

- A Surprise at the Parish House -

Justin was ready for church, but he didn't want to go. He really liked his future brother-in-law, Forrest, but the sermons were boring—at least to Justin.

I wish Mother would let me stay home today. After the wedding, I just know Claire and Mother will make me go to church every single Sunday. *But right now I just want to find Ticktock and Poppy instead of sitting for hours on a hard pew.*

He went to the parlor, where Father was enjoying his Sunday morning coffee and newspaper.

"Do I have to go to church today?" Justin asked. "I could be out looking for Poppy and Ticktock."

Father put down the paper and scrutinized his son. "Justin, Forrest is giving a sermon about telling the truth and taking responsibility for your own mistakes. You might benefit from listening."

"I know, I know. I'm trying my best to take responsibility for my own stupid mistakes." Justin sighed. He knew it would be of no use to argue.

During the church service, it was hard for Justin to keep his eyes open. It wasn't because Forrest's sermon was more tiresome than usual. It was because his message was more for grown-ups than it was for kids like Justin. Didn't ministers know that kids needed help, too?

Justin did hear one thing that stuck in his mind: Forrest said to pray for those who were unfortunate. If anyone was unfortunate, it was Poppy. Justin prayed for her while Forrest went on with his sermon. "Please help me find Poppy," he whispered.

Justin wriggled in the stiff pew. Would God, who made the earth and all the stars in the universe, hear *his* prayer? God seemed so far away. How could he hear everyone's prayers?

The sermon was finally over, and Justin and his family got up to leave. Forrest was standing on the front steps, shaking hands with parishioners. To the Butterworths he whispered, "Don't forget. You're coming over to the parish house for Sunday dinner. It should be ready now."

Oh, no, Justin thought. *I'll never get to find Poppy and Ticktock now. By the time we get through, it will be dark.*

After a few minutes of visiting with other church members, Justin and his family headed over to the parish house next door. Justin hadn't realized how hungry he was until he smelled the aroma of an oven roast drifting from the kitchen.

"Come, sit," Forrest said, his hand gesturing toward the beautifully set table. The housekeeper brought a simple clear soup in a china soup crock. Forrest ladled out the soup into small glass bowls for everyone. Justin picked his up like a cup and slurped it quickly and noisily.

"Justin!" Claire whispered. "That's rude!"

"I know," he answered. "But I'm in a hurry. I want to go look for Poppy. And my goat."

The housekeeper, who was pouring water into all

the glasses on the table, paused. "Are you looking for a goat?" she asked.

"Yes, my little goat was stolen," Justin replied.

"Well, there's a young goat tied up out in our back-yard. I wondered where it came from. Could it be yours?" she asked.

Justin jumped up and ran through the kitchen to the back door. "Ticktock!" Justin leaped off the porch steps and flew to his pet. The tiny kid bleated and her tail waved back and forth rapidly.

"It *is* you! My own little Ticktock!" Justin opened his arms and Ticktock plunged headlong into his embrace.

SUNDAY AFTERNOON,
OCTOBER 8, 1871

CHAPTER THIRTY-NINE

- *Lonely and Scared* -

Poppy was lonely now that she left Ticktock at the church. There was nowhere to go except to the ugly wooden shed where she'd been sleeping. In some ways she missed Ma's two girls. Sometimes they stood up for her, and they had usually all worked well together. Recently, though, there'd been jealousy when Poppy got the best marks in Ma's "school." Now the new girls, Julia and Renee, would take her place. She'd never be missed.

At least it was quiet inside the shed. Back at the Willow, the noisy roughs upstairs and down in the cellar rooms were hollering, fighting, laughing, and swearing all night long. Poppy was used to it. It was as Justin once said—the clocks all ticked and chimed the hours in the shop, but he hardly heard them anymore.

Poppy smelled something good—the aroma of grilling sausage! Around the corner was a street vendor who was cooking sausages and baked potatoes on a grill. Poppy gladly paid the fifteen cents for both and then went down to the waterside to eat.

The vendor had poured melted butter onto the potato and the sausage was in a roll. She tried to eat slowly, to make them last, but she was too hungry and chomped everything down in a flash.

How long could she go on with the money she had? She'd probably have to steal again. *I don't want to steal. I don't want to be Poppy the pickpocket anymore. But I'm hungry. I can't go back to Ma. No, she'll beat me for not helping her rob the Butterworths' jewelry store.*

"Poppy!"

Poppy jumped up, ready to run, when she heard her name called.

"Wait a minute!" It was Julia. "We want to talk to ya." She raced toward Poppy, pulling Renee along by her hand.

"What do ya want?" Poppy stiffened, ready for a brawl.

"I just wanted to tell ya we ran away from Ma Brennan's, too. We're wonderin' where you've been hidin' and where you get food."

"I'm not tellin' anyone where I'm stayin' and I don't have any money for food."

Julia pointed to a piece of potato skin on Poppy's dress. "So, how'd ya get that? Did you steal it?"

"No, I used the last of my money. Where are you stayin'?" Poppy asked.

Renee spoke up. "We met a lady who has lots of girls stayin' with her—kinda like Ma, only she's nicer."

"The girls are older than us," Julia said. "She says she'll put us to work someday. But for now we can stay there. It's on the fourth floor of a big house. We can see all over from our window. I ain't ever been up so high in all my borned days."

"It ain't Miss Tessie May's place, is it?" Poppy held her breath, waiting for the answer.

"Well, yeah, as a matter of fact, it is," Julia said. "Why?"

"I've heard stories about that woman. You better get out of there."

"She's been nice," Renee said. "We sleep in a real bed."

"From what I've heard back at the Willow, she's not givin' you a room 'cause she likes ya. She'll be usin' you like Ma—or worse," Poppy insisted, remembering terrible stories about Miss Tessie. "How come you left Ma, anyways?"

"Whenever we stole good stuff for Ma, she took everything we got. We can get along better by ourselves." Julia pulled a leather wallet from her pocket. "Look at this nice little boodle I fanned from a man leavin' the bank yesterday." She opened the wallet and shoved a bundle of money under Poppy's nose. "Renee's getting to be a real good little stall. She tripped and fell in front of my mark and screamed her head off."

Renee smiled happily at Julia's words.

"Yep, it was easy to lift that leather right out of his pocket while he was pullin' Renee up from the sidewalk," Julia went on. "Easy as pie."

Poppy watched Julia count the money. Although Ma had never taught her "students" to read, she had taught them the numbers on dollar bills, and they were quick to learn.

"There's thirty bucks in here. That'll keep us goin' for a while," Julia said.

"'Us'?"

"Yeah, Renee and me. We worked for it."

Poppy held out her hand. She hated to beg, but that was better than stealing, wasn't it? "How's about givin' me a few of that bundle? I ain't got any money, save a few coins. I'm not goin' to steal anymore."

"Then how do you 'spect to live? You're crazy, Poppy. Go get your own," Julia said, snapping the money out of Poppy's sight. "You know how as well as I do!"

"Don't let Tessie May know you got that money. She'll prob'ly take it, too," Poppy warned as she walked away.

Julia yelled after her, "I ain't goin' back to Ma's, so don't worry—I won't be tellin' her I saw you. But she's gonna get you, Poppy. She's mad as a hornet bee."

Poppy sighed. She'd probably have to go back to stealing in order to eat. As she walked up the streets and alleys, trying to figure out what to do, she thought of Claire. How much she wanted to be like her—at least the way she seemed to be, sweet and kind and smart.

Then she thought about Justin. Had he found Ticktock yet? She could only imagine how happy he must be. She hoped the boys really had warned Justin about Ma Brennan's threats to his goat. Did Justin now believe Poppy hadn't stolen Ticktock to get even?

She hadn't realized how far she'd gone—or even paid attention to where she was. Across the street was an empty meadow. Poppy was tired, sad, and lonely, and it was getting dark.

She trudged through the strawlike uncut hay until she found a spot that was far away from the road. She beat the tall stalks down with her feet until it lay flat. Then she flopped onto her back. A strong wind blew in gusts around her, whistling through the trees. Poppy looked up at the sky, where the stars were shining brightly.

Had Claire said there were all kinds of animals up there—bears, snakes, dogs? She squinted and tried to see them but couldn't.

Suddenly, in a burst of stardust and flame, a shooting star soared across the sky. Would that star hit the earth? she wondered. Or would it burn out up there?

Poppy didn't make a wish this time. Wishes never came true.

She closed her eyes and was soon asleep.

SUNDAY AFTERNOON,
OCTOBER 8, 1871

CHAPTER FORTY

- *Flee!* -

Justin hugged Ticktock, who snuggled under his arms, pushing gently with her little nubs of horns.

Forrest sat on the porch steps watching. "That goat sure likes you," he said, smiling. "And it looks as if the feeling is mutual."

"Forrest, will it be all right for my goat to stay here for a while?" Justin asked his soon-to-be brother-in-law. "She's in danger," he explained. "Someone in Conley's Patch wants to punish Poppy by hurting Ticktock."

"Of course you can leave her with me. I'll enjoy

having her here." Forrest reached out and petted Ticktock. "Why would anyone ever hurt Poppy or this sweet little nanny?"

"I worry about Ticktock, especially at night . . . ," Justin began.

"I'll put her in the barn at night. She'll be safe here. I promise."

Justin put his hand out. "Thank you. This goat is . . . my very best friend."

"I understand," Forrest said, clasping Justin's hand.

"I've got to find Poppy. She trusted me and my family—and we've hurt her."

"I understand that, too," Forrest said. "But for now, Justin, let it go. Sometimes when we try too hard to solve a problem ourselves, we get in the way of God's plans. Give it a rest for today."

Justin thought about this, then nodded. "I'll try to let it go—for now."

It was early evening by the time Justin and his family got home. "We should have taken Ginger and the buggy," Mother said. "The walk to church seems longer when it's dark."

"In the time it would have taken for me to go down to

Thompson's barn to hitch her up, we'd have missed the sermon today. Next time we'll go by carriage and we'll all be ready earlier," Father replied.

"Since we had such a big dinner at the parish house, I'm just making scrambled eggs for supper," Mother said. "I'm too tired to cook."

They ate scrambled eggs with ham and cheese, and then everyone, except Father, went to bed early. "I'm going to sit here and read," he said. "I'll be up a little later."

The bed felt good when Justin climbed in. And things *were* better today than they had been yesterday. At least Ticktock was back and safe at the parish house.

It seemed as if Justin had just fallen to sleep when he heard banging on the front door. Then Father burst into his bedroom. "Get up quick, Justin! The neighbors just came to warn us. There's a fire up the road and the wind is wild. The whole sky is ablaze and it's coming this way. We've got to get out of here. Now!"

It was pitch-black outside Justin's window, but when he looked out the other side of the house, he gasped. The entire sky was aflame in a whirling, twisting blaze.

"Our horse isn't here, so we'll have to go on foot.

Hurry! We've got to stay ahead of that inferno!" Charlie yelled from downstairs.

Claire was up and dressed and had a pillowcase in her hands. "I grabbed the wedding things I felt were most valuable," she said breathlessly, "along with my jewelry. I honestly don't know what's the most important—"

"Our lives are most important!" Mother shrieked. "Let's leave *now*."

"I just want to get to the church and take Ticktock with us before the fire gets there," Justin begged.

"Yes, let's head for the church," Claire agreed. "I must find Forrest and be sure he's all right. But first I've got to find Mew." She headed back into her bedroom while the rest of the family hurried outside.

Charlie ran into the barn and pulled out a wheelbarrow. "We can carry some things in this," he said.

"Have you seen little Mew?" Claire shouted from the door. "I can't leave her."

Mother raced back and pulled Claire out with her. "Never mind the kitten, Claire. Look at the fire!"

The wind blasted the flames, showering soot and sparks around them. Claire ran to the driveway. "My kitty! She'll be burned."

"She'll find a place to hide, dear," Mother consoled her. "But you can't lose your life looking for her."

"We're going now!" Father commanded. "We'll go to the shop. The fire may burn out before it reaches State Street. I've got to empty the safe with all the jewels . . ." Father's voice was drowned out by the sounds of the wild wind and the cracking of tree limbs.

It was as if the sun had risen, lighting up the neighborhood like daylight. The fiery skyline was brighter and closer.

Justin felt something hot on his face. Cinders! "Get going! Run!" he howled.

"The dry grass is catching on fire from the sparks!" Father yelled.

The family raced to the street. Charlie led the way, running awkwardly, trying to balance the wheelbarrow. Justin ran alongside him, with their parents breathlessly keeping up behind them.

Claire followed the procession. "Go to the church," she cried. "I need to find Forrest."

"Forrest has probably left the church by now," Father replied.

"No, he won't leave the church. He'll stay there until

it burns around him." Claire's voice rose to a high pitch.

"The church is on the way to the lake," Mother insisted. "We'll stop there if the fire hasn't reached it yet."

"Very well. We'll go to the church first," Father ordered. "Then I'm heading to the shop. All the jewels in the safe—they're irreplaceable."

"Your family is irreplaceable!" Mother yelled. "Which do you care about more? Your jewels? Even little Mew's life is *more irreplaceable* than those jewels!"

Justin glanced back in surprise. His mother's face was stern, her lips a straight slit. He hung back and followed his family silently. His mouth and eyelashes were dry and filled with soot from the ashes that flew in the gusty air.

"Mother!" Claire's sudden scream rang out over the wind.

Justin stopped and gasped in horror. His mother's long dress was in flames!

SUNDAY NIGHT,
OCTOBER 8, 1871

CHAPTER FORTY-ONE

- *Get to the River!* -

"Ouch!" Something hot and sharp smacked Poppy's cheek, waking her. She sat up and brushed the object from her face. "What's going on?" The sky to her left was scarlet with boiling clouds of flames and smoke. Small fires erupted in the dry grass of the meadow and were coming closer to where she had been lying. Sparks scattered and fell from the hot wind.

"The world is on fire!" She scrambled to her feet. Where was she? She hadn't paid attention when she had found the meadow.

It didn't matter. She had to get away from that terrible glowing sky and the sparks that were blowing and lighting dried leaves and trees all around her. She stumbled over the grass until she reached the road. Then she headed in the opposite direction from the fire, trying to get a sense of where she was. She remembered she had come up several side streets, so she tried to race back the way she had come.

A frightened procession of families pushed wheelbarrows filled with belongings. Baby carriages were loaded with crying children, birdcages, mattresses, and family treasures. People packed the thoroughfares and alleyways, jostling themselves and their burdens away from the blasting hot wind and flaming sky. Frantic horses driven by fear and whips wildly raced through the streets without a pause for anyone in their path.

One side roadway was so crowded that Poppy could hardly make her way through. When she finally reached the next crossing, she turned in another direction, hoping to find it less congested.

Suddenly she realized where she was! It was Justin's street, and his house was right up the road. She flew to the driveway and looked up at the house. There were no lights on in the windows. Had they left? Did they know the fire was heading this way? She had to warn them.

She ran down the driveway, and as she got closer to the house, she was comforted to see the kitchen door had been left ajar. The family had obviously left in a hurry. Poppy realized with relief that the goat barn was empty. She was about to go back to the street when she heard a familiar cry coming from the kitchen.

It was little Mew! Poppy went back to the porch, calling softly, "Come, kitty." The kitten purred as Poppy picked her up. Why had Claire left her? She'd said she'd love the kitty forever. "I won't leave you here, little Mew," she whispered gently. "You're coming with me."

A gust of wind blew the kitchen door open wide. In the light from the burning sky that shimmered through the windows, she spotted Claire's apron draped over a chair. Poppy grabbed it and quickly placed it over her head. "Now you'll feel safe," she murmured as she tucked the kitten into the front pocket.

Mew cried while Poppy ran to the street, but when she put her hand into the pocket, Mew soon snuggled down and began sucking on Poppy's finger.

Already houses behind her were in flames. The

cracking and snapping of burning wood was loud and close. Poppy coughed and gagged as smoke gusted around her. She held one hand over her face and kept one hand in the pouch on Mew's soft fur.

Once again she found herself struggling in a frantic parade of men, women, and children, who pushed and shoved and stepped on one another in their terror.

Poppy let herself be swept along in a stumbling, hysterical maze of humanity.

Now the structures around them were burning. "Help!" a man cried from a window high on the fourth floor of a nearby building. Flames spit out the windows below.

"Jump!" came calls from the street.

The man disappeared for a moment and then reappeared. He struggled with a bed mattress that he finally threw out the window onto the ground below.

"Jump!" the voices of the crowd called again.

Poppy held her breath as the man backed out the window and hung by his arms, trying to reach the windowsill of the floor beneath him. The fire was spreading and one of the walls on the side of the building was already crumbling.

"JUMP!" the crowd demanded.

He did, tumbling through the air to the ground below, missing the mattress.

Folks ran to him, but it was no use. He lay motionless.

Poppy felt sick and turned her head away. She tried to run, but it was impossible to move ahead through the wall of people.

She struggled to slip to the side of the street and stopped. A little girl was standing on the burning wooden sidewalk, screaming, "Mama! Mama!"

Her long blond hair was on fire!

"Help her!" Poppy screamed, not knowing what to do. A man standing nearby with a drink in his hand stepped closer to the girl and then threw the liquid on her.

"Stop!" his companion yelled. "That's alcohol!" In an instant the child's dress caught on fire.

Poppy put her hands over her ears to drown out the girl's screams and watched helplessly as the little girl turned into a blue pillar of fire.

Poppy felt faint. Everything seemed to be spinning. Then her legs buckled and she fell to the ground.

Someone stepped on her; a shoe dug into her ribs like

an axe. More people stumbled over her without stopping.

I must get up or I'll be crushed here. Poppy tried to push the horrible sight of that burning, screaming little girl from her mind.

Little Mew cried and was about to creep out of the apron pocket. *No! I can't let anything happen to my kitten! I've got to get up.*

She pushed Mew gently back into the pouch on the front of her apron, then tried to stand. It took several tries as grown-ups and even children pushed her out of their way, knocking her back to the hard-packed dirt street. She kept one hand over the pocket to protect Mew, but her hand was bleeding. A sharp pain shot through her right leg where someone had crushed it with a heavy boot.

One woman stopped and pulled her up. "You'll be killed if you stay on the ground, dearie," she said. "Now keep movin' toward the water. The fire won't hurt you there."

Poppy nodded and limped along slowly. The pain in her leg shot up to her hip. She could no longer hold back tears. Ma had hit her many times for crying, so she rarely cried. But now the pain was too much. She sobbed as she hobbled along, trying to hold her own with the rough crowds. With each breath, her lungs burned with the hot, fiery wind.

A large building on the other side of the street buckled under the flames and then, with a crash, collapsed into sparks and cinders.

"God help us!" someone yelled.

"Don't give up. Get to the river. Once we cross a bridge, we'll be safe!"

"That's right! Fire won't cross the water!"

"Yes! To the river!" came the cries.

Poppy felt Mew's little tongue licking her hand and then sucking again on a finger. She ignored her pain and walked faster. "Don't be afraid. We'll be safe once we cross the river," she promised little Mew.

CHAPTER FORTY-TWO

- *Stampede of the Prisoners* -

"Your dress is on fire!" Charlie dropped the wheelbarrow and, with his bare hands, began beating the tongues of flame that licked his mother's full dress.

"Be careful, Charlie!" Father tugged off his jacket and wrapped it around Mother, finally smothering the flames.

"Are you burned?" Father asked anxiously. "Are you hurt?"

"No, just singed a little. I'll be all right," Mother said in a trembling voice. "Did you burn your hands, Charlie?"

"Not badly." But Justin saw that he cringed when he took hold of the wheelbarrow again.

"Even though the fire is still behind us, the sparks and flames are blowing in the wind," Father said. "So watch out for sparks on your clothing."

"More fires are starting everywhere with this gale." Claire pointed to a building where dark smoke had suddenly burst into flames.

"We've got to get to the lake," Charlie suggested. "The fire will have to stop once it reaches the shoreline."

"Sure, it'll stop when it gets to the water—but we could be driven into the lake," Father said. "We'd be safer heading across the river."

As they continued their flight, hundreds of people crowded the streets.

"Where are my children?" a woman screamed. "I can't find them!"

When they approached the Methodist church, Claire heaved a sigh of relief. It was still unharmed, although the roof of the parish house was smoldering.

"I'm going for Ticktock!" Justin yelled over the chaos as he raced to the barn in the rear of the parish house. "Charlie! Help me open the door," he called to his brother.

Charlie set the wheelbarrow down and followed Justin to the barn.

"Help me lift the board that's holding it closed," Justin hollered.

Charlie looked at his hands and shook his head. "My hands are blistering," he said. But he took one end of the board and lifted it.

Once the door fell open, Ticktock came running out. "Here, here, Ticktock," Justin said, grabbing her. "She's frightened of the fire and the noise."

Charlie found the broken clothesline and tied it to the goat's collar. "Where's the family?"

Claire was clinging to Forrest, who had appeared from the side of the church. "Please come away with us," she begged. "Down to the river or the lake."

"No, I can't leave. One of my parishioners, Mr. Haskell over there, says he can save the church if he can keep the roof and steeple wet. He's going to climb up, and we'll have a pulley of water from the well. Those men are helping." He pointed to a group of men who were pumping water into pails. "Darling, you must get away now," he said to Claire. "Get to the water where you'll be safe."

"I don't want to leave you."

"You *must* leave now." Forrest's voice was commanding. "Please, before it's too late."

"The fire's still roaring," Mother said as she looked up at the smoldering garnet sky. "Why haven't they put it out?"

"There aren't enough men or horses in the world that could put this fire out. Look at the skyline!" Charlie said. "This isn't a fire. It's an inferno!"

Forrest kissed Claire and then pushed her away. "Go, now! I'll find you once it's over. I promise." He turned and rushed to the men who were waiting with water buckets. Mr. Haskell was already climbing up to the roof.

"Come on, Claire!" Mother begged, pulling her daughter by the sleeve. "We've got to keep ahead of the fire."

"State Street's on the way to the bridge, and if the fire hasn't hit yet, I can remove the jewels," Father said.

Mother's voice rose to a scream. "For the last time, forget the jewels!"

"Those jewels are—"

"I know! *Irreplaceable!*" Mother stomped furiously out to the street, ahead of everyone.

Claire said nothing but followed her mother. Justin, with Ticktock on the rope leash, ran after them.

"Wait! We need to stick together . . . ," Father called.

Charlie shoved his father out onto the sidewalk. "For God's sake, get going!"

For a moment, even in the midst of the terror, Charlie's words to his father shocked Justin. But this was no time to think about good manners.

"Where are you, Mother?" Justin called as they became swallowed up in the streets that were overrun with shoving, screaming people. Wild-eyed horses reared and their wagons tipped over. Furniture, pets, paintings, musical instruments, and other prized belongings spilled onto the ground, cluttering the pathway of the frightened crowds, who trampled over them.

Ticktock was clearly terrified and tried to run and jump away. Justin lifted her up and carried her until the trembling stopped and the goat nestled in his arms.

The family was now close enough to State Street to hear the fire signals from the courthouse building. "Listen!" Father exclaimed. "The fire alarms are sounding one after another."

Suddenly the whistles were silent. "What happened?" Claire asked.

"There's smoke coming from the courthouse roof! I

thought that building was fireproof," Charlie declared as they approached State Street.

"Nothing in this stinking town is fireproof," Father hollered. "It's all wood, with fake stone facades and brick."

"That's where the fire alarms sound," Mother said. "And now that the courthouse is on fire, the alarms are burned out."

"What about the prisoners?" Claire asked. "The jail is in the courthouse. They'll burn to death in there."

"There's your answer!" Mother pointed to a stream of men in striped prison suits who raced out of the building, then broke into different directions, darting down the street, laughing and cheering.

"We're free!" they yelled.

"Break into the saloons and we'll celebrate!"

One man grabbed a chair that had been left behind on the street and smashed it. Grabbing a broken chair leg, he ran to the department store in a nearby building, broke the front display windows, then climbed through the broken glass.

Outside a music store, a piano stood where someone had tried to save it. A prisoner jumped on the keyboard, then leaped to the top of the expensive instrument and waved his arms. "This fire is a blessing from heaven for the poor among us. Grab whatever you want." He jumped off the piano, kicked down the door of a nearby store, and disappeared inside. In a moment he emerged with his arms full of clothing.

A woman whom Justin had seen in the crowd suddenly broke away and headed to an expensive fabric store across the road. Others followed her.

Two men who were hiding inside blocked their way. "You can't come in here like thieves!"

The woman pushed them aside, and the others behind her punched and clobbered the men who were trying to protect their property.

Within a few seconds, the woman came out carrying a huge bolt of costly silk. Others raced out of the smoldering building lugging sewing machines, bolts of cloth, and furniture.

Smoke streamed from the broken front window of a shoe store. One of the released prisoners rolled up a newspaper, lit a match to it, and tossed it through the window. Instantly the smoke inside burst into flame.

"They're lighting more fires," Mother said in disbelief.

"I'm going to our store. Mrs. Palmer's emerald is in the safe. It's priceless. You come along, Charlie and Justin. We've got to protect what we own."

Mother stomped her foot. "Absolutely not! Let those thugs and rowdies take what they want."

"It's our livelihood, woman, and we're going to the shop!" Father took hold of Charlie's arm and pulled him toward the street.

"Go ahead, then," Mother snapped, "but you're *not* taking my sons into that danger. And if you do, don't come looking for me after this is over. I won't forgive you. Ever."

Justin looked at his mother in astonishment. Never had he heard her speak that way. The fire seemed to have brought out an inferno that was smoldering within *her.*

Father was stunned, too, as he stood there with his mouth open, at a loss for words.

After a moment, Claire put her hand on her father's shoulder. "Father, dear, what Mother said is right. I know it's hard to leave everything behind. It hurt me to leave Forrest. But surely you wouldn't take Justin and Charlie into that conflagration." She kissed his cheek. "And Father, you mustn't go either. What would we do without you?"

Father was silent, his face illuminated by the flickering of the fiery sky. Then he nodded and motioned for the family to move on.

Justin set Ticktock on the ground again and they continued their trek toward the water, dragged along by the massive crowd that surged around them. He wondered about Poppy. *Where are you, Poppy? Are you safe?* He wished more than ever that he could ask her for her forgiveness.

But he now believed in his heart that he'd never see her again.

CHAPTER FORTY-THREE

- Poppy Picks a Pocket! -

Poppy was swept along the wooden sidewalks, not knowing where she would end up. Her throat ached with the heat of the air and wind, which carried the flaming sky.

The people were frightened and shouting. Animals, too, were caught up in the crowds. Panic-stricken horses reared, kicked, and turned in every direction, looking for a way out of the turmoil. Dogs howled and bit anything in their paths.

Poppy soothed the little kitten deep in her pocket,

patting her gently. She thought about Ticktock and hoped the little goat was safe and not frightened. She knew Justin would be gentle and loving to his goat, just as surely as she cared for little Mew.

As Poppy moved with the crowds, a sudden explosion burst in the distance. *What was that?* she wondered. The answer came quickly when the gas streetlights fizzled and went out.

"The gas tanks exploded. That's what the noise was!" a man yelled.

The boiling, burning sky still lit the streets and the crowds moved on, away from the fire. But the fire continued to follow them.

Now Poppy approached an intersection that was familiar. State Street! On the other side of the street was the Butterworths' jewelry store. Although the fire was spreading, it seemed that the flames had not yet reached that far.

Her heart skipped when she saw men coming out of the store. Was it Mr. Butterworth and his sons? She realized in the glow of the fiery sky that the front display windows were broken. Thieves had broken into the store and were stealing the Butterworths' property.

"The courthouse is burning down!" someone yelled. "The prisoners are in the streets!"

"They're breaking into the stores! They're like wild animals!"

Poppy wiggled through the crowd and ran across the road, ignoring the sharp pain in her leg. When she approached the jewelry store, she saw men in prison uniforms helping themselves to the watches, brooches, and cuff links in the now-broken glass showcases.

Was there anything that she could save? Someone had kicked the front door open and Poppy slid inside. No one paid any attention to her as thieves pulled clocks and paintings from the walls.

What about the jewels and the safe in the back? she wondered. *Have they found them yet?*

Three men were fighting over a wall clock.

"Get your filthy hands off this timepiece," one of the wild-eyed convicts yelled.

"I saw this first, and I'm takin' it," another criminal shouted.

The third man, who was not in prison garb, was trying his best to pull the others away from the beautiful mahogany wall clock with its fancy gold numerals and hands. With a powerful blow, he hit one of the others in the face and the clock crashed to the floor. The chimes inside clanged noisily.

Poppy wanted desperately to run and save it, but already the third man had scooped it up and was running for the open door. The other two thieves dived at him and the ruckus continued.

Poppy crept behind the counters and into the office. The safe was there, but the door was broken—apparently forced open with a crowbar that had been dropped beside it.

She groped inside the safe, hoping the velvet bag was still there. But the safe was empty. The jewels were gone.

Poppy glanced around in the darkness. Everything had been taken. As the room lit up with flickers from the approaching fire, she knew she had to leave.

In the showroom, more men had come in, grabbing things from one another, punching, beating. The smell of alcohol was strong, so she knew the thieves had been drinking, which added to their ferociousness. She'd slip out the door and hope they didn't see her.

Poppy made her way cautiously around the brawling men, moving slowly around the perimeter of the room, and stopped suddenly. A man in the middle of the melee wore jeans and had a large knapsack attached to his back.

Poppy noticed that the man had something sticking out of the sack. In the glimmer of the firelight that flashed through the window, it looked like the drawstring top of the velvet bag of gems. Could it be?

Mew began crying and clawing to get out. *Not now, Mew!* Poppy stuck her left hand down and wiggled her finger into Mew's open mouth. *Hold on just a little longer, kitty!*

Poppy crawled noiselessly in the shadows, getting closer to the drunken men. Could she lift that bundle out of the man's backpack without his knowing? Every muscle in her body tightened as she watched for the right moment.

Back and forth the men stumbled and kicked. Other rowdies and convicts cheered them on from the door.

Poppy crouched next to a showcase, trembling. She had to stay calm and remember all the things she knew about picking pockets.

One of the convicts pummeled the man in jeans, knocking him against the counter where Poppy was hiding. As the drunken man threw himself back into the fracas, Poppy reached out for the velvet bag. She knew she couldn't touch *him* or he would certainly catch her.

Poppy's nimble and deft fingers lifted the bag from the sack in one easy tug—just as another of the fighters pounced on him.

"Get that bum!" one of the roughs yelled.

Poppy froze. Was he shouting at her?

"Take that, you pig!" came another shout and a loud smack. "That clock goes with me!"

Straightaway, Poppy stuffed the velvet bag into the pocket with Mew. The kitten began to cry again. *Hush, Mew! Don't make a sound!*

Poppy moved quickly and quietly. The men were so violent and engrossed in their fight that they didn't notice Poppy creeping through the darkness to the back of the store. She reached the back room and sneaked to the outside door. It was locked but she felt for the key, fumbling in the dim light.

Her fingers found the key—it was in the lock just as she remembered. *Hurry! Hurry! Before he finds out that the bag is missing!*

Her hands quivered as she turned the key. The door opened and Poppy ran out into the backyard. Trees and grass were already on fire, and flames twisted in the wind. She dashed around the building and back into the street, hoping that the man inside had not noticed the bag of gems was gone.

Hurry! Mew's cries seemed louder and louder.

Pushing the ache of her injured leg from her mind, she made a beeline across the street to the surging mass of terrified people. No one noticed little Poppy as she pressed herself into the mob. Soon she was lost in the seething crowd, who thought of nothing else but escaping the fire.

When she felt safe enough, she reached into her pocket and lifted the bag away from Mew, who was clawing and crying.

The bag was heavy and lumpy with the gems inside. Poppy could hardly believe it. In her hands she was holding the sack full of precious jewels.

CHAPTER FORTY-FOUR

- Blame and Regrets -

Justin stood on tiptoe to see over the crowd in front of him. "The bridge! It's just ahead of us. We'll be safe soon."

As they approached the State Street Bridge, Charlie groaned, "The fire has crossed the river! The buildings over on the other side are burning."

"Oh, look at the boats—they're on fire," Justin said gloomily.

Father threw up his hands helplessly. "The oil and all the junk on the surface of the water acted like fuel."

"I told you we should have turned down that side

street a few blocks back. Then we'd have gone down to the lakefront," Mother said in an accusing voice. "No one listens to me!"

"That's all we do is listen to you," Father snapped. "You never stop talking."

"This is no time for 'I told you so,'" Charlie scolded. "We'll cross the bridge. No more discussion."

They continued being swept along by the crowd, climbing over the bodies of dead animals and abandoned carpetbags, steering clear of wandering horses and wheelbarrows still filled with belongings. Some people stopped long enough to pick through the items and take what they wanted.

"Thieves everywhere," Father muttered.

Suddenly Charlie set down the wheelbarrow that he'd been pushing for hours. "I can't do this anymore! My hands are so badly burned—my blisters have broken and now they're bleeding. Can someone else push this? Otherwise, I'm leaving everything right here."

"I'll take it," Father said. He placed the bag he was carrying onto the top of the overloaded barrow and began pushing awkwardly as the top-heavy cart wobbled in every direction.

"Leave it," Mother told him.

"I'll try to get it over the bridge," Father insisted. "If I can't, I'll leave it."

"We're not moving," Charlie said. "Everyone is funneling onto the bridge."

Justin stood on his tiptoes and looked ahead once more at the slow-moving wall of people. All the while the surging, towering flames and turbulent clouds of smoke roared skyward.

Justin felt trapped. Perhaps they should go back to that street his mother had said led to the lake. He stood tall and stretched to see behind them. Another barricade of people!

Suddenly, for a fleeting second he saw—or thought he saw—a small familiar figure struggling in the midst of the crowd. *Is that Poppy?* It was hard to tell in the darkness when the only light was from the fiery sky. Whoever it was disappeared from sight.

Justin turned around as a wagon made its way through the mob. "I have room for your belongings," the driver called out. "Twenty dollars and I'll carry your things to Lincoln Park and meet you there. That's where everyone's heading. The fire hasn't touched the park."

"Over here!" Father called. "Take all this stuff in the wheelbarrow."

"Twenty dollars cash now," the driver said.

Father pulled out his leather and handed over the money. The driver hopped down from the cart and tossed everything from the wheelbarrow into the back of the wagon.

"Take this, too," Mother said, throwing her stuffed pillowcase to the man.

"What about your bag?" the driver asked Claire.

"No. I'll keep this with me," she answered. She looked guiltily at her mother. "My wedding linens are in here," she whispered. "They're the only things I could carry." Her eyes filled with tears.

"It's all right, dear," Mother said, and patted Claire's hand.

"Hey, kid," the driver said to Justin. "I'll take your goat if you tie her into the bed of the truck, but it'll cost another ten dollars."

"No!" Justin picked up Ticktock and cuddled her. "She stays with me."

Nearby, a large man yelled at the driver and the Butterworths. "Move! The fire's headin' this way, for the love of God!"

The driver climbed into the cart and clicked the reins, and his horse tried to move through the line of people. "Get outta the way!" he hollered. Then, brandishing a whip, he cracked it over the heads of those in his path.

The crowd opened up and Father urged the family on. "Now we can move faster."

"How are your hands, Charlie?" Mother asked.

"Sore—real sore. But I can't think about it now. Let's just get to Lincoln Park and meet the driver."

"I heard some of the crowds are heading to a cemetery up there," Father said. "There are few trees in the park and cemetery to catch fire."

Justin set Ticktock down and the family continued across the bridge. The air was hot and Justin wished he had drinking water for himself and for his pet. "Can we get water?" he asked.

"There should be water soon," Father said. "The new water tower is on this side of the river. The water tower is built of limestone blocks. It can't burn down."

"But there's only one waterworks and that has a wooden roof," Charlie said.

"Look!" A woman nearby pointed to the fire that had now taken hold on the far side of the river. "It's heading that way. And if it hits the waterworks, there'll be no water to drink—and none for the fire engines."

"What fire engines?" another woman said mockingly. "Half of them are broke, they've been so overworked. I heard they've even misplaced some of the horses! We've got a bunch of stupid idiots runnin' around loose." She spit on the ground. "Chicago will be wiped right off the map."

"It's all punishment from God," the first woman said. "This city is the most wicked city in the world. The fire is an act of God."

Justin spoke up. "We live here and we're good people. Why would God punish us?"

"God isn't punishing *anyone*," Claire said. "It's a *fire*. That's all."

Justin thought about Claire's words and felt better. If God had caused this terrible fire, well, Justin would never go to church again—even if Forrest was preaching.

They were off the bridge now and onto a street on the north side of the river. Then Justin thought of Poppy. "I think I saw Poppy back there in the crowd," he said to Claire.

"You did? I hope she's safe," Claire said with a trembling voice. "I want so badly to let her know I trust and believe in her."

"We let her down, didn't we?" Justin said.

"Remember that night when she was trying on the dress? Poppy broke down, wanting so badly to live a good life. I said I'd help her. Oh, Justin, she looked up at me with those big brown eyes and . . . I know she believed everything I said and promised." Claire began to weep again. "I shall never forgive myself if anything happens to Poppy."

"Neither will I forgive myself," Justin whispered.

EARLY MONDAY MORNING,
OCTOBER 9, 1871

CHAPTER FORTY-FIVE

- *Terror!* -

Poppy at last crossed the bridge, still clutching the heavy velvet bag under her arm.

What time was it? she wondered. It was hard to tell with the flames and smoke whirling and twisting overhead. But the sky was bright enough to light the way. So far she had had no choice but to be carried along by the others who were also fleeing from the fire.

The pain in Poppy's leg was now unbearable, and every step felt as if a butcher knife had cut her leg muscles. When she lifted her dress to look at her injury, she realized how badly she'd been hurt. Her leg was bleeding from a deep wound.

If only she could find water so she could wash the cut and get a drink. Her mouth was dry and she tasted cinders and ash. To add to her fears, she was afraid something was wrong with Mew, who cried constantly.

She spotted a woman who was drinking from a jug of water she had hidden under her cloak. Poppy limped over to her. "Please, ma'am, can I have just a drop of water?"

"No! If I give you water, someone else will be wanting it." Then her voice softened. "There should be water nearby. The water tower can't burn down."

"Please, could you put a drop on my finger for my kitten?"

"Your *kitten*! Now I've heard everything." The woman snorted and turned away.

"Wait, look!" Poppy begged. She opened her apron pocket and pointed inside. "I've carried my kitten all this way, and now I'm afraid she'll die if she doesn't get . . ." Her eyes filled with tears, and little Mew began another series of yowls.

The lady peeked inside. "Oh, my, child, there really *is* a kitten in there!" She looked up at Poppy. "Where's your ma?"

"I don't have one. There's just me and my kitty."

"Come here." The woman pulled Poppy gently under her shawl and opened the jug. "Have a good drink, child."

Poppy shifted the heavy bag of jewels under her arm. Then she drank from the jug that the lady held to her lips. Poppy let the water stay in her mouth for a moment before swallowing it, then took another gulp. "Thank you, ma'am," she whispered.

"And here's some for the kitten." The woman cupped Poppy's hand and poured a trickle into her palm.

Poppy carefully held her hand down to Mew, who licked the water eagerly.

"Thank you," Poppy said, smiling gratefully at the kind woman, but tears were spilling down her cheeks. "My leg's hurtin' so bad. I just want to stop somewhere and sleep. I can't go on anymore."

"How'd you hurt your leg, child?"

"It got crushed when I fell. Someone stomped on it. I know once I stop walkin' I'll never start again." Poppy was sobbing now. She didn't care what Ma would have said. She didn't even care if she made it to safety. But she did care about Mew, who had stopped crying and was sucking Poppy's finger again.

"Poor little things—the both of ya," the woman said. "Let me take a look at that leg."

Poppy sat on the side of the road with the bag in her lap. She lifted her dress while the woman bent down to look. "Oh, my good Lord," she said. "You got yourself a bad cut that needs to be stitched up, girl." She got up and opened the jug of water again. Then she tore a piece of cloth from her petticoat. "This is 'bout the cleanest bandage we can get today."

Poppy gritted her teeth as the lady washed her wound with the rest of the water in the jug. Then she wrapped the white cotton cloth around Poppy's leg and tied it with a piece of twine from her bag. "I hope it stays on. I can't tie it too tight—that would hurt you more."

"It feels better now." Poppy impulsively threw her arms around the woman. "Thank you. Please stay with me."

"I can't, honey." The woman stood up, unwrapping Poppy's arms from around her neck. "I've got to keep goin' and I'll be walkin' too fast for you with that leg. I got to get to Lincoln Park. I think that's where my girls have headed."

The lady was about to move on but paused, eyeing

the velvet bag in Poppy's lap. "If you got something important in there, you should put it into something less noticeable. Here." She pulled a heavy paper bag from her satchel. "That velvet pouch will draw attention. Some thievin' rascal would grab it in a second. I'm surprised you still have it." She unfolded the bag and held it open while Poppy placed the velvet pouch into the paper one.

"Get along to safety, child. God bless you and your kitten." The woman turned and walked ahead until she disappeared in the crowd.

Poppy got up, tucked the bag under her arm, and moved on. As she hobbled along the road, she noticed a tall building on the next block with smoke coming out of the windows. Suddenly, with a loud blast, the smoke burst into flame. Soon screams came from the open windows.

When Poppy approached the building, she saw that a narrow plank of wood had been set up from the fourth floor of the burning structure over an alley to the fourth floor of the building next door. A woman with a child in her arms was slowly crossing on the plank, one foot in front of the other, to the waiting hands in a window on the other side. Cheers went up when she made it.

"That's Tessie May's building," Poppy heard someone say.

"They can't come down the stairs 'cause the lower floors are burnin'," another person added. "Let's pray that board holds!"

Julia and Renee are living in that place! No sooner had Poppy thought about her friends than she saw Julia tottering high on the wooden plank.

Be careful, Julia. Go easy! Don't fall!

Poppy held her breath as Julia moved slowly and cautiously across the board. She heaved a sigh of relief when Julia made it safely into the open window on the other side.

Now Julia was leaning out the window, waving for someone else to follow her. Renee!

Renee screamed and kicked as a woman lifted her and placed her out on the flat timber. In the building opposite, Julia climbed out the window and back onto the plank and motioned for Renee to come to her.

Renee nodded, and then, with her arms outstretched, she began the trek to her friend.

Below, Poppy watched in fear. The crowd stared silently as the little girl teetered on the narrow board.

Then Renee looked down at the alley. She stopped in panic, crying and trembling. The board itself shook and the child fell to her knees, her hands grasping the edges of the plank.

Julia was crying, too, as she began crawling toward Renee. Suddenly the board dipped in the middle, and each end pulled free of the windows.

Down the two girls fell—Renee first, then Julia! Poppy saw them silhouetted against the scarlet sky, their arms and legs flailing, as they dropped down to the alley.

The board flipped over and over until it hit the ground with a loud thump.

All those watching screamed and sobbed. "Oh, those poor children."

"Isn't there someone here who can see if they're still alive and need help?"

Poppy was stunned and couldn't speak or move. As if in a dream, she observed the woman who had helped her heading toward the alley. A few others followed.

"Watch out! The fire's spreading!" someone called. The grass in the alley flamed up from dropping cinders.

Poppy turned away and headed up the street. She didn't want to see or know anything more about Julia and Renee. They were gone. And that was it. She was too weary to cry anymore.

Poppy walked away, dazed, knowing only that she must flee. How long she'd been walking, she didn't know or care. She vaguely realized that dawn was starting to break and Lincoln Park was just ahead. She hobbled into the dried grass of the park, hearing the constant wail of the wind mixed with cries of distress, while the blazing fire raged on.

I must get to the water. Run away . . . far away . . .

Crowds were camped on mattresses and in makeshift tents. She stumbled around them. Then faintly—like distant music—she heard someone call out, "Poppy! Poppy!"

Her knees buckled and she was about to fall when she felt someone's arms encircling her.

"Our little Poppy!"

She heard nothing more.

CHAPTER FORTY-SIX

- At Lincoln Park -

It seemed to Justin that the whole world was burning. Now they were on the north side of the city, and still the whirlwinds shot the flames up to the sky, twisting and boiling.

"We should have gone to the lakeshore," Mother complained. "We'd be safe at the waterside."

"No, ma'am." A gentleman who was trudging along nearby spoke up. "Some of the city folks crossed over the river and went down to Michigan Avenue and the lakeshore. They're all trapped down there."

"Then we should have gone to the prairie—to Grandpa's," Justin said.

"Most everyone from the north side is already up there. But anyone on this side of the city can only cross the river at the Twelfth Street Bridge now. There's no other way."

"So we'd be heading back into the fire if we headed for the prairie," Father said.

They entered the park from the south entrance. "There must be thousands of people here," Justin said in awe. "Where should we go?"

"There's a line," Father said, pointing. "Perhaps there's water over there."

They reached a fountain where water was still running. Several policemen guarded it and provided tin pails for those who had no way to collect the precious resource.

Ticktock cried when she saw the running water. "You can't water animals from this fountain," the police officer told him. Justin filled a pail, drank from it eagerly, and then filled it to the brim again before leaving the line.

Justin and his family moved away, each carrying a pail of water. "Over here," Father suggested, finding an empty spot on the grass. Once there, Claire opened up her pillowcase and pulled out a folded sheet that had been hand-embroidered with blue forget-me-nots and daisies. "This is a gift from Randy's mother," she said. "She worked on it all summer." Claire unfolded the sheet and spread it on the dry grass. "It'll be put to good use right now. We'll claim our spot with it—and we'll all sit down and rest at last."

"First I'm going to give Ticktock a drink." Justin set the pail in front of his goat and watched as she lapped up the water eagerly. "You've been such a good little kid," Justin said. "You haven't complained, and you've kept up with me all the way."

"She is a sweet thing," Mother agreed as she sat wearily on a corner of the sheet. "And you've taken good care of her, Justin."

Claire spoke up. "I only wish I could have saved Mew. I can't bear to think of her in that fire. She was just a baby—too small to fend for herself." Her eyes filled up and she turned away.

"Some things had to be sacrificed," Father said, heaving a sigh. "I have to admit I was foolish to even consider going back to the shop. Our lives are worth more than all the jewels in the world." He sat close to Mother and put his arm around her. "This is the most difficult time we've been through as a family. We may have to start all over, but . . ."

Mother put her head on Father's shoulder. "At least we're still alive and together."

"And if we could withstand this fire, we can withstand anything!" Charlie said.

"How are your hands now, son?" Father asked Charlie.

"I washed them. Wish we had something to put on the sores."

"Once the blisters break, they can become infected," Mother said. "If that driver would only bring our belongings! I have clean clothing in there that we could use for your hands."

"From what I've been hearing, I doubt if we'll ever see our things again," Father said. "Men with wagons are charging to cart things for a price—and then they go around the corner and dump them. Then they start over with another poor sucker."

"I have clean cloth for Charlie's hands," Claire offered. She opened her bundle of wedding linens and handed her mother a pillowcase. "Tear it up and use it for bandages."

"Oh, no, Claire," Charlie objected. "It's for your trousseau."

Claire hugged her brother. "Haven't we learned that *things* don't matter?"

Father stood up and glanced at the line for water. "The police are sending people away. I wonder why?" The family watched as Father went to the fountain and talked with the officers there. He came back, shaking his head. "The water works burned down and the water can't be pumped. I don't know how much worse it can get."

"It's almost dawn. And the fire's still roaring over there." Mother nodded toward the west. "If only the wind would stop."

"If only it would rain," Charlie said.

Mother sighed and ripped the pretty pillowcase into strips. "Come on, son, let's protect your wounds."

When they were finished, Charlie laughed and held up both hands, which were fringed with embroidery. "I'm sure I have the *prettiest* bandages around."

Now that dawn was breaking, they looked around for familiar faces.

"Look who's coming this way!" Father exclaimed. "It's Dr. Anderson!"

The doctor waved hello as he approached the family. "So glad to see you made it!"

He glanced at Charlie's hands. "I do have my medical bag here if you need anything."

"Broken blisters—I'll be all right," Charlie said. "I'm sure there are other folks who need your help more than I do."

"This fire is a tragedy beyond belief. There are wounded folks out there not far from this park." Dr. Anderson gestured to the flames that were shooting up into the sky. "It's raging beyond control, and it's next to impossible to get in there to save anyone."

"I hear the cemetery is full. And they're still pouring into this place." Father looked toward the south entrance. "Why, that little girl . . . she looks familiar."

Justin followed his father's gaze. A child in tattered clothing staggered into the park. Her face was stained with soot, and her eyes stared ahead as if she was in a daze. She struggled with what seemed to be a heavy bag and she kept the other hand in a front pocket.

"Is that . . . Poppy?" Justin asked.

Claire jumped up. "Yes! Yes! That's my apron she's wearing! Of course it's Poppy!"

"Poppy! Poppy!" Justin called. "It *is* you!"

Poppy looked around aimlessly.

"Oh, Poppy, darling," Claire called as she and her brother raced toward her. "Oh, thank you, God. Thank you!"

"Poppy, Poppy," Justin sobbed and tears dripped down his face.

Poppy's legs buckled under her, but not before Claire caught her in her arms.

Claire held her close and covered Poppy's sooty face with kisses. "Our little Poppy," she whispered.

CHAPTER FORTY-SEVEN

- *Promises* -

"Poppy, darling!"

Am I in heaven? Is that an angel calling me?

"Poppy, wake up." Someone was crying.

Maybe I'm dead. Slowly Poppy opened her eyes.

Claire was holding her, rocking her. "Oh, my sweet Poppy. To think you went through all this *alone*."

"I . . . I wasn't alone. I had Mew." She tried to sit up. "Oh, where's Mew?"

"Right here." Justin held the kitten up. "She's fine, Poppy. You saved her."

Is Justin crying?

"The bag . . . where is it?" Poppy mumbled.

Claire looked around. "Over there, on the ground. It dropped when you fell."

"Don't lose it . . . Don't let anyone get it. . . ." Poppy strained to get up again but fell back into Claire's lap, sick and dizzy.

"It's all right, Poppy—it's right here." Justin picked up the paper satchel from where it had fallen and handed it to her. "It's heavy. You carried this all the way?"

Poppy nodded. "It's for your father," she whispered.

"For me?"

Poppy looked up and realized that Justin's whole family stood around her with anxious faces.

Justin handed the satchel to his father. Mr. Butterworth looked puzzled as he reached inside and pulled out the velvet bag, and then he gasped. "The jewels!" Father opened the bag, then poured the gems onto Poppy's lap. "They're all here, including . . ." He plucked Mrs. Palmer's emerald from the pile. "I can't believe it!"

"I didn't steal 'em, I swear," Poppy struggled to explain.

"Of course you didn't," Claire said, kissing her on the cheek.

"When I got to State Street, the pris'ners were runnin' wild, breakin' into the stores and takin' things. I saw the broken windows in your shop, so I went over to see."

Poppy stopped in a fit of coughing.

"Here, Poppy." Mrs. Butterworth held a pail of water up to her lips. "You don't need to explain, dear. Just rest."

But Poppy needed to tell the Butterworths what had happened. After she sipped the water, she went on. "Inside, the men were fightin' over the clocks and one of 'em had this velvet bag in his knapsack. Justin once showed me the jewels in that bag, so I knew they belonged to you." She stopped and looked up at Justin. "Oops. I'm sorry, Justin."

"It doesn't matter if he showed you the jewels, Poppy," Mr. Butterworth said. "I'm thankful that he did!"

"But how did you get the bag from the thief?" Charlie asked.

"While he was fightin', I reefed it from him."

"You *reefed* it from him?" Father shook his head and chuckled softly. "You picked his pocket?"

Poppy nodded.

"It's a wonder you got away alive, my child," Mother said in horror.

"It was dark and no one saw me. Besides . . ." Poppy looked down. "I'm a really *good* pickpocket."

Father quickly gathered the jewels and put them back into the bag. Then he took Poppy's hand. "Little girl— little Poppy. You could have lost your life to save those jewels for us; there you were, so brave as you struggled through that fire all alone and thinking we never believed in you." To Poppy's astonishment, Mr. Butterworth's eyes filled with tears.

"It's all right, sir," Poppy said gently. "I knew ya would've had trouble believin' in someone like me. But I never did steal that chain or whatever it was you thought I'd taken."

Claire drew her close. "We've wanted to tell you how sorry we were that you overheard us that night—"

Justin interrupted. "It was all *my* fault. I didn't want to get blamed. . . . Aw, Poppy, I'm so sorry."

Mr. Butterworth put his hand on Justin's shoulder. "I know how much you want to be included in our business, my boy. And you felt left out. Now that we have the jewels, thanks to Poppy, we can start over again—

and things will be different. You'll see. After all, we're a *family*."

"And that family includes *you*, Poppy," Claire promised.

"Indeed it does," Mr. Butterworth agreed.

EPILOGUE

- *Solid Gold* -

Three months later, Poppy stood in the vestibule of the Methodist church waiting for the organ to begin the wedding march. Two large bouquets of flowers rested on a table. Sunbeams danced in rays that poured through the windows, making patterns on the hardwood floor.

Claire looked like a princess in a white satin dress, her blond hair piled high and braided with pearls, a sparkling sapphire brooch—designed by her father—at her neckline. Poppy caught sight of her own reflection in the glass door to the sanctuary. Her bridesmaid gown was dark red velvet and trimmed with ivory lace. A crown of pearls and red roses adorned her chestnut hair that curled almost to her waist.

I feel as if I came out of the fire brand-new!

The fire had burned itself out that Tuesday morning in the park, thanks to a cold, cleansing October rain that had fallen gently on Poppy's face. The Butterworths had all been there, watching over her and caring for her and loving her.

After the fire, Poppy stayed with the Butterworths at the farm on the prairie, which had been spared. The big white house in the city along with the sweet little goat barn were gone.

The family was already constructing another home where there would be a new shed for Ticktock and a barn for Ginger. The people of Chicago were quickly rebuilding their city—and Butterworth's Jewels and Timepieces on State Street would soon be even larger and more impressive.

Poppy never knew what became of Sheila or Noreen, but she heard that Ma Brennan had been thrown in jail for twenty-five years for looting. She'd never trouble Poppy—or Ticktock—again!

Mr. Haskell was able to save Forrest's church by keeping the roof wet and pouring water down the steeple. The parishioners had already rebuilt the parish house. Claire was excited about moving into her new home, and since Claire and Forrest planned to adopt her, Poppy—and Mew—would live with them.

"Imagine, we'll have our first child—and she's twelve years old!" Forrest had said, laughing.

"Will Poppy be my sister or my aunt or my cousin?" Justin asked when he heard the news.

"She'll be your *niece*. You'll be her uncle," Father explained. He gave Poppy a hug. "But she'll be *my* granddaughter!"

"And mine, too," Mrs. Butterworth reminded him.

Now at the church, Justin, Charlie, and Mr. Butterworth tiptoed into the vestibule.

Justin held a white package tied with a gold ribbon. He handed it to Poppy. "This is for you."

Poppy untied the ribbon and opened the cover. Inside, a golden flower with a bright ruby in the center hung from a gold necklace. She removed the necklace and held it in her palm, where it shimmered in the sunlight that filtered through the windows. "I ain't never seen anything as pretty in all my borned days."

"It's a *poppy*. Charlie and I designed it together," Justin said. "I'm glad the wedding was postponed a month so we could finish it."

Claire put her arm around Poppy's shoulder. "It's solid gold—just like you!"

"The gold flower shows it was your strength and courage that got you through the fire," Mr. Butterworth explained.

"The ruby in the center was my idea," Justin said proudly. "It represents the flames from the fire. The ruby is one of the gems you saved, so it really *did* come through the fire, and it's only right that you should have it."

"Did this ruby come from way down under the earth?" Poppy asked.

"Yes," Claire told her. "Yet, see how brightly it shines."

"Poppy," Mrs. Butterworth said, "let me fasten your necklace." Poppy lifted her curls as Mrs. Butterworth secured the chain.

Mrs. Butterworth took her sons' arms and smiled up at them. "Are my two boys ready to usher me down the aisle?"

The young men escorted their mother to the front row

of the sanctuary, where she and Justin took their seats. Then Charlie, as best man, joined Forrest at the front of the church.

The organ music burst into the wedding march. Claire picked up her bouquet of white lilies and took her father's arm. They'd walk together, but Poppy would go first.

All the guests stood and looked to the back of the church where Poppy waited with her own bouquet of red and white roses.

Whatever happened to Poppy the pickpocket? Justin wondered as Poppy smiled from the vestibule doorway. *Everyone and everything has changed for the better since the fire,* he realized. *Or really, since the day Poppy crashed into me as I swept the sidewalk.*

Poppy fingered the solid-gold flower that hung from her neck.

"Go on, Poppy, you're next," Claire whispered.

The music swelled. Poppy took a deep breath, and the brand-new solid-gold Poppy started down the aisle.

AFTERWORD

The Great Chicago Fire of October 1871 is known as one of the greatest disasters in American history. The fatalities are estimated at 200–300 souls. Considering the powerful firestorm that destroyed the city, this was thankfully a small number of people.

The fire obliterated an area of about 2,000 acres including more than seven miles of roads and 120 miles of sidewalk. You'll recall that in the story the sidewalks were made of wood. The city lost 17,500 buildings. The Chicago Water Tower, which was new at the time and was built of limestone bricks, withstood the fire and still stands as a memorial of this disaster. However, the roof of the nearby pumping station collapsed and it became impossible to pump the water into the firemen's hoses.

What caused the Chicago fire? Certainly not Mrs. O'Leary's cow, as the old story goes. But the fire did start at the O'Leary's house.

What made it a firestorm? There was a terrible drought in that area of the country for several weeks. Chicago used wood for everything, including the sidewalks and buildings. Lumber companies were dry as tinderboxes. This setting made perfect conditions for an inferno. The wind gusted to hurricane force, spitting sparks across the parched ground and woodlands. Whirling tornados of fire spiraled skyward. To make matters worse, the wrong alarms went off. Horses and firemen were exhausted from fires that occurred the day before. Finally, when the fire destroyed the pumping station near the Chicago River, there was no way left to fight the fire. People ran to cemeteries and to Lincoln Park, where there were no buildings, for safety— just as Poppy and Justin did in my story.

Did you know there were three other huge fires on and around the shores of Lake Michigan on October 8, 1871—the very same day as the Chicago Fire? The

Peshtigo Wisconsin Forest Fire—sometimes called the "Forgotten Fire"—which took place 250 miles north of Chicago, is considered the "greatest forest fire disaster in our nation's history." It is estimated that between 800 and 2,500 people were killed. The same day, on the eastern side of Lake Michigan, the town of Holland went up in flames. About 100 miles north of Holland, the town of Manistee, Michigan, was badly destroyed by a fire that is now known as the "Great Michigan Fire." To the east, on Lake Huron, yet another conflagration burst through Michigan's "thumb," destroying Port Huron.

One day later, on October 9, the city of Urbana, Illinois (south of Chicago) was badly damaged by fire. And on October 12 a fire swept through Windsor, Ontario.

Here's a fascinating theory of what might have caused all these fires in this area of the continent: Eyewitnesses of the Great Chicago Fire confirmed they had seen "shooting stars" and believed the inferno might have been caused by a meteor shower. From their viewpoint it is reasonable to surmise that burning meteorites might have sparked off fires on the tinder-dry areas.

In 2004 engineer and physicist Robert Wood suggested—based upon the eyewitness accounts of balls of fire, spontaneous ignition without smoke, blue flames falling from the sky, and the fact that four fires had blazed around Lake Michigan on October 8, 1871—that the root cause could have been the methane gas found in comets. To add to this premise, Biela's Comet was actually breaking up over the Midwest at that very time in October 1871. And now you know why Poppy got to see the shooting stars.

Although my story is fiction, the historical facts concerning the fire are carefully researched and the story is woven around the history, rather than vice versa. Here are some of the interesting true facts that are mentioned in this book:

There really was a place in old Chicago called "The Willow" where the real Roger Plant offered criminals a place to work and hide and party.

It's been said that the word "underworld" (meaning "criminal world" or "gang center") came from the empty foundations that were left when the Chicago lawmakers of that era ordered all buildings to be lifted up from the swampy ground on which they were built. These dank, dark foundation walls were often used as hideouts by criminals.

Mary Brennan really existed and had a "school" for girls where she taught them to steal and pick pockets. The girls had to give all the money they stole to Ma Brennan. She rewarded them with penny candy.

When the fire reached State Street, the criminals held in the courthouse jail were set free. With the fire raging close by, they immediately began to vandalize and steal from the shops, including a jewelry store.

While there were other fires to choose as a background for this book, I was fascinated by the many unique and extraordinary characters in Chicago at that time. That's the reason I chose the city of Chicago and the Great Chicago Fire for the setting of my story.

KEEP READING FOR A LOOK
AT ANOTHER NOVEL FROM
JOAN HIATT HARLOW!

It's summer 1942, and Jill and Wendy have both been sent to Maine because of World War II. Little do they know their summer is about to be anything but boring, because this is one town with a few too many secrets . . . just waiting to be uncovered.

"I don't think Aunt Adrie knows him," Wendy said. "At least, she's never mentioned him to me."

"Maybe she was ordering squab for the inn," Jill suggested. "She said she'd be starting meals soon. Clayton Bishop said he raises pigeons for food."

"Perhaps so. You don't need to use ration stamps for pigeons," Nana said. "But if you're hungry, you'd probably need to eat four squab. There's hardly any meat on them."

Jill shuddered. "I've never eaten a pigeon and I don't think I ever will—even when they're called *squab*."

"Oh, but I've heard they serve them at all the ritzy restaurants," Wendy said.

Nana reached for a potato chip. "Jill, tonight's my night out. Every Sunday night I meet with friends. I'm hoping you'll be able to keep yourself busy on Sunday evenings without me."

"It's okay, Nana. I listen to my favorite radio programs every Sunday. I'll be fine."

Nana nodded. "Good."

"I love Charlie McCarthy!" said Wendy. "He's on Sunday nights."

"What do you do with your friends?" Jill asked her grandmother. "Play cards?"

"No, we just talk," Nana said. She got up and took the empty plates from the table and headed inside.

"Can you come over on Sunday nights?" Jill asked Wendy.

"Right after I help with the dinner dishes." Wendy heaved a sigh. "There's only Aunt Adrie and me right now. I hope we don't have too many guests at the inn this summer. I don't want to miss the clambake and the dances coming up." Wendy looked over Jill's shoulder. "Say, look who's come to visit."

Quarry MacDonald was standing in the driveway by his bicycle. "What's he doing here?" Jill whispered.

"He's probably following me," Wendy answered under her breath. "I told you he likes me."

Quarry waved and adjusted the kickstand on the bicycle. "Hi!" he said, coming into the yard. "Just thought I'd drop by to say hello." He sat down on the picnic bench. "Guess I missed lunch—and me hungry enough to eat a boiled owl."

"Too bad," Jill said.

Quarry ignored her comment. "Hey, what are you two doin' tonight?"

"Why?" Wendy asked.

Quarry spoke directly to Jill. "I know your grandma meets with the other witchy ladies on Sunday nights, so I figured you'd be alone and wonderin' what to do."

Jill frowned. "What do you mean, 'witchy ladies'?"

"That's what everyone calls 'em. They have secret meetings at Ida Wilmar's house. No one knows what's goin' on. It's been kinda suspicious for round about a year now."

"What do you mean *suspicious*?" Jill demanded. "Can't some ladies get together and knit or something without the whole town wondering what's going on?"

Quarry shrugged. "Word gets round this town. Lots of blabber mouths in Winter Haven."

"The ladies are probably knitting afghans. All the club women back home are making afghans for servicemen,"

Wendy said. "There must be enough afghans for everyone in the world by now."

"Don't forget Bundles for Britain," Jill added. "My mom keeps a big barrel in the garage and we fill it every month with clothes and blankets to send overseas."

"Oh well, it's no one's business what those ladies do, anyway," Wendy said. She turned to Quarry. "What are *you* doing tonight? Jill and I thought we'd listen to Charlie McCarthy. Want to come over?"

"Is it okay, Jill?" Quarry asked.

"I guess so," Jill said reluctantly. "I'll have to ask Nana first."

"Ask me what?" Nana appeared from the house with more dishes and a pie. "Dessert is ready. Hello, Quarry. Want a slice of apple pie?"

"Quarry wants to listen to the radio with us tonight while you're gone," Jill explained. "Is that all right, Nana?"

"It's fine by me." Nana slid pieces of pie onto the plates. She handed Jill a wedge of Gouda cheese and a knife. "Cut this up four ways," she said. "It tastes good enough to eat, with apple pie."

"I'll do it," Wendy offered, slicing the cheese and placing a piece on each plate.